The Haunting Of Laurilee Inn

By TrishAnn Williams

Fire Opal is an imprint of Parker Publishing Inc

Copyright © 2011 by TrishAnn Williams
Published by Parker Publishing Inc
12523 Limonite Avenue, Suite #440-438
Mira Loma, California 91752
www.parker-publishing.com

All rights reserved. This book is protected under the copyright laws of the United States of America. No part of this publication may be reproduced, stored in a retrieval system, or transmitted in any form or by any means—electronic, mechanical, photocopying, recording, or otherwise—without the prior written permission of the publisher.

This book is a work of fiction. Characters, names, locations, events and incidents (in either a contemporary and/or historical setting) are products of the author's imagination and are being used in an imaginative manner as a part of this work of fiction. Any resemblance to actual events, locations, settings, or persons, living or dead, is entirely coincidental.

ISBN: 978-1-60043-109-8
First Edition

Manufactured in the United States of America
Cover Design by Parker Publishing Inc

Chapter One

Beth Willis stirred restlessly in her sleep as the temperature in the house dropped several degrees. Her eyelids twitched in REM state as she dreamed.

In her mind, the dream was real.

It was 1881 in Atlanta, Georgia. The woman stared out the window. Long, gnarled fingers pulled at the tattered shawl draped around her shoulders which did little to keep out the chill from the winter air. She breathed in shallow gasps from ribs visible through her plain cotton dress. She had been beautiful once; but, now, olive skin hung loose and gaunt on her thin frame and her thick dark hair had turned prematurely gray.

Rats scurried in and around the trash bins lining the alleyway outside her window; but, the woman didn't feel the cold or see the alleyway, dirty and drab, in front of her. In her mind, she stood at the third floor window of a grand home, looking out over the grounds below. Just beyond the house, tendrils of smoke curled from the chimney of the kitchen as dinner was prepared and, even farther, she could see the edge of the cotton fields. Out of sight, but visible in her mind, were the slaves' quarters where her family lived after spending twelve hours a day in the fields. She knew she was lucky.

A shout of laughter grabbed her attention and the woman shifted her gaze to the courtyard below her. Two children engaged in a hearty game of tag held her interest. Tears welled up in her eyes as she watched them. They were beautiful children with laughing eyes and bright smiles. Like hers, their skin was olive and healthy and they both had full heads of black hair. Although their mother liked to proclaim proudly that the children looked exactly like her, this woman knew that was impossible. Those were her children and, no matter what it had cost her, she knew that bringing them into the world had been the right thing to do.

The woman blinked in the harsh sunlight streaming through the dirty windowpane and brought her mind back to the present. It had been many years since she had lived at the grand house. Every day she sat at the window, waiting for him to come and get her and bring her home. Back to Latte Plantation and her children. When she returned, she would be able to hold her babies like she was never able to do when they were young. Only then would she find peace. Her fingers clenched and unclenched as she struggled for breath that became increasingly painful.

Her mouth uttered the prayer that had been her comfort for so many years, "Praise the LORD! Praise, O servants of the LORD, praise the name of the LORD! He gives the barren woman a home, making her the joyous mother of children. Praise the LORD!"

As she closed her eyes for the final time, she vowed with the last remnant of her strength to find her children and bring them home…

Beth sat straight up in bed, her heart pounding wildly and her body covered in a thin film of sweat. Her hair, damp and matted, clung to the back of her neck and each breath quivered with a rawness that felt like she'd been crying.

She blinked and tried to focus her eyes in the unfamiliar room. The thick darkness surrounding her, pressed against her as shadows leapt from every corner. Outside, something sinister screamed in the night. She cowered in the massive four-poster bed, gripping the sheets to her chin. Her eyes were wide and scared, frozen by fear.

As her breath began to slowly even out, the shadows retreated into outlines of furniture that she was not yet accustomed to and the gentle rustle of trees outside the window replaced the sinister screams. Her heart slowed into a more rhythmic pattern.

Calmer now, Beth sat up in bed and took a couple of deep breaths to gather her wits. She was in a new environment. Sleeping in a different bed. Living in a hundred year old home that had stood vacant for years. Surely, it was not unexpected that she would have a restless night every now and then.

But the dream…

It had felt so real.

Beth pushed herself off the bed. Her feet touched the wood floor with a solid thump and she reached for the slippers lined neatly against the edge of the bed. The room suddenly felt ice cold and she grabbed the thick robe she had discarded before bed hours earlier.

Leaving the chill in the bedroom, she crossed the hallway to her office and stood before the window overlooking the courtyard below her. The first orange-pink rays of daylight peeked over the horizon in a breathtaking display. The courtyard was designed to be a haven for guests when her bed and breakfast opened the following week. It was a peaceful place with lush landscaping and comfortable benches for reading or relaxing.

Beth blinked and, in her mind's eye, saw the courtyard the way it had been in the dream--a grassy area where the children played.

Beth stepped back from the window. There was no mistaking the place in her dream. It had been this window and this courtyard, and it had been filled with sadness.

Shaking her head, Beth pushed away the thought and moved out of the room. It had been a dream. Nothing more.

Right now, she had a full day ahead of her.

She had a bed and breakfast to open.

Beth believed that fate had taken her off the freeway on her way to Atlanta that particular day just two months ago. She had been looking for a gas station; but, as she passed by the old plantation house, something had called to her--something beyond the overgrown yard and peeling paint. Instead of stopping for gas, she had made her way directly to the real estate office listed on the faded for sale sign. From the moment she stepped foot inside the house, she had known her instincts were correct. The house pulled her in, comforting her with its grand entrance and solid bones. It had been beautiful once, she could tell even in its neglected state, and she had known without a doubt that it would be her destiny to restore that house to its former glory.

Beth felt a tug at her heart. If only it were that easy to spruce up the human soul. Like the house before her, Beth had seen her share of neglect over the past couple of years. The sudden death of her parents had shattered everything she took so easily for granted in her life. Although she had been left financially independent, she felt hopeless and lost. Until now. She felt a connection to this majestic, abandoned house. Turning this house into a successful bed and breakfast was her purpose.

"And it is going to be magnificent," she announced with determination, "as soon as I figure out what to name it." With her grand opening in less than a week, she had yet to officially christen her new business. Her current reservations, taken from her internet web site, were listed simply under the name Garden Ridge Bed & Breakfast, derived from the name of the small town in which the Inn was located. But, that wouldn't do. A place this important deserved a name that carried all of the dignity and elegance that the house itself possessed.

As she crossed the hall back to her bedroom, Beth tried several names out loud.

"Bay Breeze." She shook her head. Too commercial.

"Morning Glory." She frowned. Too corny.

"Beth's Bed and Breakfast."

Laughing aloud, Beth tossed her robe on the bed and gave up for the moment. Sooner or later, the exact right name would come to her.

Beth's private suite took up the entire third floor. It might have once been a floor for children, for a large open room occupied almost half of the floor which seemed to indicate the former presence of a game room or nursery. Beth was using it as an office. Across the hall, a cozy sitting room connected to a large bedroom and bath. She didn't have the luxury of a veranda, as did the second floor, but the view up here was spectacular nonetheless.

After changing quickly into jeans and a t-shirt, Beth moved to the vanity, which had been left behind by the previous owner, to check her reflection. The mirror was three-paneled, old and starting to blacken around the edges. A silver brush and comb set, also original to the house, was the only adornment on the top of the vanity. Beth reached down to touch the tarnished metal.

A chill moved through the room.

"Darn it." Beth shivered and reached for a sweater she had already had to use several times since she moved in. "I have got to get the air conditioning looked at again," she reminded herself, although the only place she really seemed to have the problem was on the third floor.

By the time she shrugged into the sweater, the temperature seemed to have righted itself again. She sighed and shook her head. It was an old house after all; she supposed it had the right to be temperamental.

Back in her office, Beth moved to the window and looked out over the lush green lawn sprawled out before her. It was such a peaceful setting and Beth thought she would be very happy here.

"Laurilee."

"What?" Startled, Beth turned from the window, expecting to see one of the construction workers lurking in the background. But, they were done with the third floor; and, as she suspected, she was completely alone.

She cocked her head, listening hard. There were no sounds.

Beth turned back to the window, thinking maybe she had heard a gust of wind through the trees outside. But, the leaves on the trees were still and unmoving.

"Hmmph," she said aloud, curious, but not overly concerned, "must have been the house settling."

Shaking off the odd feeling, Beth moved to her desk, where her project list sat waiting.

An hour later, Beth looked up from her list of potential names, frowning, as a whisper breezed through the air like a puff of smoke.

"Laurilee."

Rising from her desk, Beth pulled her sweater tightly over her chest. Again, the room felt cold. For the second time in an hour, Beth made a quick tour of the third floor, checking the rooms and, for the second time in an hour, found absolutely nothing out of place.

She returned to her desk and the list she had been working on. The house had been formerly known as the Latte Plantation named after the original owners. She was trying to keep something from the history of the house in her name, but, so far, nothing seemed quite right. She went over the list for what felt like the hundredth time.

LP Bed & Breakfast

Magnolia Place

Laurilee Inn

Beth stopped, staring at the sheet of paper before her. Her mouth formed a small O of surprise. She hadn't written that last name.

She held the paper up. There was no mistaking the precise curves of her handwriting. She closed her eyes briefly and opened them again. It was still there. Bold and beckoning from the center of the page.

"You have got to be kidding me," she said aloud. What was going on here? This could no longer be considered a coincidence.

"Laurilee," Beth tried the name aloud. Her voice boomed across the empty room and she jumped a little. An instant later, she whispered, "Laurilee."

Taking a deep breath, Beth looked up at the ceiling as if it would provide answers. Laurilee.

She shook her head. The word had no significance to her. She didn't know anyone named Laurilee. In fact, she was certain she had never heard the name before.

Why had it come to mind so suddenly? And how did it end up on her list of names for the Inn?

Beth closed her eyes for a moment. She must have heard it somewhere. The word must have some subconscious meaning to her; a character on a soap opera or a name in the newspaper. But, somehow she knew that it was no coincidence. The name Laurilee had some significance. She felt it in her heart.

She dropped her eyes to the list of names again.

"The Laurilee Inn," Beth said the name aloud. Her heart pounded, not in a frenzy, but with excitement. She couldn't explain it. At least not yet. But, it felt right.

"Okay," she announced aloud. "You win. I officially pronounce this house the Laurilee Inn."

In response, Beth felt a calm, peaceful silence throughout.

Just after lunch, Beth decided to head down Main Street for an afternoon walk. It was a lovely day in Garden Ridge. Not quite summer, which would be stifling, but sunny and bright with just a nip of coolness left over from winter.

Breathing in the fresh air, Beth strolled along the street. A block or so later, Beth noticed a faded sign in front of an old Victorian house that read "Library".

Beth stood on the sidewalk, placed her hand over her eyes to block the glare from the sun, and took a good look at the sprawling house before her. As was the case with most of the houses in town, this one appeared to have been quite grand in its day, with its towering peaks and ornate decorative gable trim. Unfortunately, now, the paint was faded and several pieces of the elaborate trim were missing or broken. On the other hand, the grass looked recently mowed and the porch housed a white hanging swing that looked comfortable and inviting. The structure was a study in contradictions that made Beth instantly curious.

She took a step inside the wrought iron gate surrounding the property. She was curious about the house itself, but also about what kind of information might be contained within. From the looks of the outside, it wouldn't surprise her if the library didn't house a book newer than 1980. On the other hand, the information she was interested in dated far earlier than that. Her curiosity about the house she had purchased had grown immeasurably since the previous evening. She felt certain there was a connection to the name Laurilee and she wanted to know what it was.

Peering suspiciously through the open doorway, Beth took a step inside. The foyer was dark and dusty. There was no information desk. No bell to ring. No indication of life whatsoever.

Beth walked hesitantly toward the first open door to her right. The house was eerily quiet and she walked gingerly so that her tennis shoes, soft-soled as they were, made no sound on the wooden floor. She poked her head through the open door to discover what was formerly the formal dining room. The furniture had been removed, but an elaborate chandelier hung from the ceiling. Bookshelves lined the walls and several books lay open on a small table in the center of the room.

"Hello?" she called, backing out of the room. Her voice bounced off the walls and came back in a resounding echo.

Tom Hartman raised his head as the echo reached his office. He had been staring at the blinking light on his answering machine for the better part of a minute. He knew the message by heart for he'd been sitting in this very spot when the phone rang. He'd heard clearly the urgency in his agent's voice asking, no, begging, really, for him to pick up the phone. After a long and painful length of silence, Tom heard the audible sigh of resignation followed by the brief message indicating that his deadline was now two months overdue. Tom shifted his gaze back to the computer screen in front of him. It was blank.

Tom sighed.

What good was it to be the most famous ghost novelist in the country if you couldn't write a ghost story?

"Hello?"

There is was again. While he had a fairly steady stream of local clientele that flowed through the library each day, such a greeting was most unusual. He had a very open policy at the library; and, in the event he was writing, rare as it was, most of the locals preferred not to disturb him. They knew that eventually Tom would wander downstairs to catch up on local gossip and whatnot and were content to browse in silence until that happened.

But, today's voice sounded unfamiliar. It was only one word, but Tom thought he detected the slightest bit of an accent. He thought it might be British.

Either way, this development was intriguing enough to rouse Tom from his thoughts and he rose from his desk to make his way downstairs to the library. He didn't give a backwards glance at the blank screen on his computer, jeering at him in its silence or the blinking light on his answering machine, waiting to be played.

Back in the foyer, Beth continued her inspection. The next room she entered, originally a study, contained bookshelves stained a deep mahogany and built in to the walls. A beautiful antique desk occupied one corner of the room along with three or four dark leather chairs. It was a masculine room, overflowing with books, both on the shelves and stacked along the floor. This place seemed to be in desperate need of some filing.

Beth walked to the nearest bookshelf. For grins, she removed a book and opened to the title page. Copyright 1971.

Just as she suspected. She slammed the book shut and returned it to its place.

Then she stopped, staring at the title of the book she had grabbed. *The Five Levels of Ghost or Paranormal Activities.*

Without thinking, she reached for the book again and opened it to the beginning. At the top of the page in big bold letters was the statement: Level One: Sense Attack

The list was extensive and included such items as: feelings of being watched, odd odors and smells, and hearing footsteps.

Beth started to close the book when the next sentence caught her eye. Ghosts are sometimes accompanied by a feeling of cold, either by a drop in the room temperature or an icy breeze or wind. Beth raised an eyebrow. She had certainly experienced enough cold spots in her house recently.

Curious, she flipped to the next Chapter: Level Two -- Communications. She unconsciously held her breath as she read though the list: hearing voices, strange noises, whispers, giggles or laughs. The ghost makes it presence felt -- can no longer be confused with tricks of the mind.

"May I help you?"

When the deep, masculine voice reverberated through the room, Beth jumped guiltily, dropping the book to the floor where it bounced with a loud clatter.

"I'm sorry, I..." she stopped as she turned and gazed into a pair of alluring gray eyes, framed by thick dark lashes. The kind of lashes that most women would kill for. But, instead of lending any sort of feminine air, they only accented the structured line of his jaw. What was this beautiful man doing in a small town library? Flustered, she cleared her throat and said, "I'm just looking for a book."

Tom felt his heart flutter for a second. Her slight English accent had not been imagined. It had a soft, seductive lilt that he found extremely attractive.

He nodded and smiled. "Looks like you're in the right place." He offered his hand. "Tom Hartman."

She returned his grip with a soft, but firm, handshake. "Beth Willis."

As her eyes met his with a clear blue intensity, Tom's heart skipped a beat.

While Garden Ridge boasted its fair share of available women, this particular one was like no one he had ever seen before. Her copper hair fell over her shoulders in long ringlets secured by a white ribbon. Her skin gleamed smooth and fair in contrast to her dark hair. She was tall and slim and graceful. Absolutely stunning.

For a moment, he was afraid he saw a glimmer of recognition in her eyes; but, just as quickly, she returned her gaze to the room, taking in the clutter of books.

Tom let out an instinctive breath of relief. She didn't seem to recognize him.

A lifetime ago, in another world, he was almost always recognized.

Closing his eyes for a moment, he forced himself to remember that he had shed that image two years ago. As long as he was in Garden Ridge, he was just Tom.

Tom stepped forward again and asked, "Is there something I can help you with?"

Beth picked up the book she had dropped and replaced it in exactly the position she had found it, despite the disarray of the rest of the room. She stepped away from the shelf behind her and asked, "Do you have any idea where the librarian might be? I have quite a few questions."

Tom laughed and responded, "At your service."

Beth paused for a moment and then turned back to him. "I'm sorry?"

"I'm the librarian," Tom stated clearly.

Beth froze in her place. He was the librarian? She took a closer look at the man standing before her. He wore a starched button-down shirt and crisp blue jeans. His sleek jaw was clean-shaven and his jet black hair smoothed away from his face in thick waves. Tom

Selleck without the mustache came to mind. Still, that hardly made him a librarian. A movie star, maybe....

Smiling at her obvious discomfort, Tom asked, "You were expecting someone else?"

"Well, yes," she stammered.

He raised an eyebrow, waiting for her explanation. But, what was she going to say? That he was too good-looking to be a librarian? That was just ridiculous.

Beth cleared her throat, annoyed at herself for being flustered. She was a grown woman. So what if the man looked like a movie star? That didn't mean he couldn't love books.

"I'm sorry," she said, "it's just that…" She stopped, thought for a moment, and then asked, "You're really the librarian?"

And they were back to square one.

Tom laughed, a deep rumble that came from the heart. "I'm actually the librarian by default." He looked around the room and then back at Beth. "It's my house."

He saw her expression of surprise and curiosity, but he didn't elaborate. When he had taken up residence permanently in Garden Ridge, this old abandoned library had served as a refuge. A place for him to write the next great novel. He had moved in, occupying the second floor, but made no changes to the original layout of the first floor.

He had never officially reopened the library; but, as often happens in a small town, people stopped by to visit. Kids needed books for school. Grownups with projects around the house or mysterious ailments that needed curing. So, little by little, over the years, the library took on its own informal shape and Tom unofficially became the town librarian.

Sometimes, especially once the writer's block set in, it was much more fun being a librarian than a professional writer. So, while his book gathered dust in his private office, he installed computers with Internet connections and started a weekly story time for the kids. For the most part the house remained lost in the past, more of a place for people to gather than a wealth of information; but, he did his best, and the people around town seemed to appreciate it.

Beth watched the emotions flicker across Tom's face. A little nostalgia. A little sadness. And then a smile of resignation. It felt intimate to Beth and, for a split second, she wanted to reach out and touch his hand in comfort.

But, just as quickly the expression dissolved and Tom offered her a warm, friendly smile. A glowing, radiant flash of white teeth and the shadows disappeared. He clapped his hands together and announced, "So, what can I do for you?"

He was an intriguing man, Beth thought. She would bet her bottom dollar there was a lot more to this man than just the easy-going librarian on display right now. She had a feeling that he was a man full of surprises... and secrets. On the other hand, who didn't carry a secret or two around?

She met his smile and proceeded with the purpose of her visit. "I'm looking for some information on the house I just bought."

Tom nodded. "Is it haunted?"

Beth's heart skipped a beat. She narrowed her eyes suspiciously, "What makes you ask that?"

Tom was a little taken aback by her response. He had been joking, but he could see a sudden flush in her cheeks that wasn't there before and she watched him with wariness. As if the subject made her uncomfortable.

Tom shrugged easily, but watched her closely, as he replied, "You are in the paranormal section. It was just a guess."

"Oh," Beth regarded him with continued misgiving, and responded cautiously, "No, it's not haunted."

Tom was pretty sure he heard her add, under her breath, "I don't think."

"Okay," Tom's interest was definitely piqued, but he ignored the muttering and asked instead, "So, which house are we talking about?"

"810 Main Street," she replied. "It's the white colonial at the top of the hill."

"I know the one," Tom replied agreeably. "I can access the county courthouse on my computer upstairs. We should be able to gather some tax information, which should have a history of ownership in no time. That would be a good place to start."

"That would be great." She studied the staircase dubiously and then turned back over her shoulder, asking, "Are you sure you don't mind?" She certainly didn't want to take advantage of the man's kindness.

For the briefest moment, Tom thought about the blinking light upstairs on his answering machine. His agent was probably furious. But, really, couldn't that call wait just a little longer? After all, Tom had nothing new to report. His deadline had come and gone months ago. His saving grace was that his last novel, now two years old, was still on the bestseller list. He still had time. Besides, whether it was the mention of ghosts or the slight hesitation in her eyes or even just the fact that a very attractive woman was standing in his foyer; whatever the motivation, Tom felt strongly that he needed to get to know Beth Willis a little better.

Now he smiled and raised his hand toward the staircase, "I don't mind a bit." His grin was open and friendly, like he didn't have a thing to hide. He looked around the empty room. "It's not like I have much else to do."

"Thank you," she replied and followed him up the stairs to the second floor.

Tom's working office was small and cluttered. He immediately began shoving together stacks of paper in order to make room for Beth to walk behind the computer desk which faced a large bay window overlooking Main Street. Beth could see her house standing majestically in the distance, which made her smile.

Tom sat down and began typing. Within seconds, the whir of the computer booting up filled the room.

As the computer whirred and processed, Beth glanced furtively around the room. Much like the library downstairs, Tom's private office appeared to have a cluttered sense of organization about it. She noted that the computer was state of the art, as was the printer set up alongside it. Stacks of paper lined both the floor and the credenza behind the desk. And a bookcase full of books occupied one entire wall. Beth stretched her head to the side just a tad to catch a glimpse of the papers stacked nearest to her.

It looked like a copy of a magazine article or a page from a newspaper or something. She shifted her gaze a little to get a better view of the title.

Reincarnation: its meaning and consequence

Beth blinked and commented lightly, "That's some interesting reading material you have."

"What?" Tom looked up from the computer screen. He followed her gaze to the article on this desk and then immediately stiffened. "Oh, that," He quickly snatched the stack of papers from the desk and shoved them in a desk drawer. "One of the library patrons sent me that – I haven't had time to read it yet."

His voice was perfectly light and calm, but Beth sensed he was lying. She was instantly curious as to why.

She adopted the same calm tone, leaning casually against the desk. "Are you interested in reincarnation?"

Tom didn't move his gaze from the still-blank screen as he shook his head. "Not particularly."

Lying again. This man was a mass of contradictions. She shrugged. "It's just such an unusual topic for someone to send a random article."

Tom shrugged. "I'm the librarian. People send me random articles all of the time." But the tone in his voice clearly said back off.

Beth flushed, feeling she had gone too far. Fortunately for her, the computer beeped loudly and the blank screen suddenly filled with writing. She moved her gaze back to the computer and said quickly, "Oh, look, our information is up."

Tom felt a stab of guilt at her obvious unease. He hadn't meant to snap at her; but, he felt vulnerable here in his office surrounded by his work--his real work. He was afraid that she would uncover his true identity and he wasn't ready to reveal that information.

He gladly took the opportunity to focus his attention at the screen before him. Tom read aloud, "Looks like the house was built in 1857 by Mr. James Latte."

"Yes," Beth agreed instantly, "It was known as the Latte Plantation – it was a cotton plantation."

"The cotton plantations of that era were magnificent," Tom concurred and then added, "You know, many owners at that time also raised the crops and livestock required to support the plantation. The plantation would have originally contained a separate wash house, the original kitchen, a barn or two, probably a smokehouse, cotton house and maybe even a blacksmith shop. The plantation communities were completely self-sufficient."

As Tom spoke, Beth's memory flashed back to her dream the other night. There had been other buildings behind the house. The kitchen with long tendrils of smoke curling from the chimneys. The carriage house full of hay for the horses and the stables where they were kept.

"Oh," Beth raised a hand to her lips as the vision careened through her mind like a freight train, overloading it with visual images. The force of it buckled her knees and she lost her balance.

"Are you okay?" Tom reached out to touch her shoulder and Beth started.

Stepping back and moving her hand from her mouth to her chest to cover her racing heart, Beth said, with just the slightest shake in her voice, "Yes, of course."

But Tom noticed the tremor and watched her with interest. "Is this the kind of information you were looking for?"

"Not really," Beth admitted, but then amended quickly, "Although the history is fascinating. It's part of why I'm so drawn to the house. It seems to have such a presence about it." As the words left her mouth, Beth shivered and she looked away. The house did have a presence--a life of its own. The question was--whose?

Tom noticed the shiver and the change in her expression. He responded with a serious tone. "They do, don't they? Almost as if each owner leaves a little piece of themselves behind."

"Yes," Beth said, a little too loudly. That was exactly what she had been thinking. A little bit of someone had been left behind. A little bit of Laurilee.

She turned to Tom with a new sense of urgency. "Can we find out more about them? The Lattes, I mean?"

Tom heard the frenzy in her voice and refrained from answering for a moment. Her sudden, almost desperate, interest seemed completely out of character from the cool, collected woman of only moments ago. What had rattled her so?

Deciding to play along for the moment, he suggested, "Well, you could check the State Records Department. They would have records of any marriages, births, deaths… that sort of thing."

Beth's eyes grew wide with excitement. "Can you do that from here?"

Tom shook his head. "I'm afraid not. It's in Atlanta."

Her face fell and he took pity on her. Springing to his feet, he snapped his fingers and said, "You know what? I think I saw a history book of Garden Ridge somewhere just the other day. Let me think…"

Like a whirlwind, he left the office, ran downstairs and began searching briskly from room to room. Beth struggled to keep up. Finally, in the back section of the ballroom, Tom stopped, bending down to sort through several stacks of books lined up on the floor. He would pick up a book, study it for a moment, cock his head to one side in thought and then toss it carelessly into another stack.

"Shouldn't you be more careful?" Beth couldn't help but ask. She was certainly no expert, but those books appeared old and fragile to her.

"Yes, I should," Tom agreed instantly, just before tossing another book aside.

Beth raised an eyebrow, but didn't comment.

A moment later, he issued forth a triumphant "Ah, ha!"

Tom held up an ancient book, using both hands. In gold letters on the spine were the words: *Garden Ridge: 1800-1980*.

Tom took the book to the nearest reading table. Beth followed close on his heels. Opening the book to the 1850's, the two began searching for the familiar name: Latte.

"Here it is," Tom noted after a moment.

Sure enough, a two-page article with the heading, James Latte, jumped out from the worn, yellow page. A blurry, black and white, photo occupied one side of the page. Beth leaned in and squinted at the picture. Mr. Latte appeared to be a small man with dark hair and a thick mustache. Next to him was a big-boned woman, also with dark hair and very masculine features.

Beth touched the pictured and whispered, "What was his wife's name?" She felt sure it would be Laurilee or something similar.

Tom scanned the page. "Malthilde. Or Mattie it looks like they called her."

Beth frowned, "Malthilde?" Not even close.

Tom misunderstood her frown. "You don't like the name?"

Then she sighed and whispered, "It's just not what I was expecting."

Tom gazed at her with open curiosity. "You were expecting something?"

Beth laughed self-deprecatingly. Good point. What was she expecting? Some mysterious link to the past? Some super natural influence? She was being ridiculous. Still...

"Did they have children?"

She tried to move the book out of Tom's grasp, but he held tight. "You didn't answer my question."

She met his gaze, feeling stubborn. "Answer mine first."

Tom gave her an exaggerated frown. "But, I asked first."

"I know," she replied, giving the book a tug so that she could get a better view of the book. She skimmed the pages quickly, all too aware of Tom's gaze on hers. He leaned to peer at the words over her shoulder. So close that she could feel the warmth of his breath on her neck. He smelled sweet, like wintergreen. Was it gum or mouthwash? What did it taste like?

She swallowed thickly, suddenly distracted. How had her thoughts just wandered away like that? She turned the page with an unsteady hand, staring at the words which suddenly made no sense. All she could feel was the nearness of Tom Hartman.

"Here." His deep voice cut into her daydreams.

She blinked and followed his index finger as he skimmed a paragraph near the bottom of the page. "Two children-- a boy and a girl," he continued reading, "Jonathon and Samantha."

He leaned back and asked, "Closer to what you were looking for?"

With some distance between them, Beth felt a little more in control. He just smelled so good.

She shook her head and finally digested the new information. Jonathon and Samantha. Two children. No Laurilee.

She smiled with just a trace of disappointment. "I was hoping I'd run across the name Laurilee." She offered a weak smile. "That's what I'm naming the bed and breakfast. The Laurilee Inn."

Tom smiled, open and friendly. "That's a nice name. Does it have any particular significance?"

How could she explain the breeze? The whisper? He would think she was nuts. Anyway, she was no longer even sure of what she felt. No wonder she hadn't found any link to the history of the house. It had just been her imagination in the first place.

Shaking her head, she smiled at Tom. "No significance; just a feeling."

"Well, I like it." Tom grinned and closed the book.

Beth smiled back. He was so friendly. He was impossible not to like.

As they walked back to the foyer, Beth stopped in front of the main book room, her mind flashing back to *The Five Levels of Ghost or Paranormal Activities*. She turned to Tom, "You asked me before if my house was haunted. Do you know much about the subject?"

"Haunted houses?" Tom asked, stalling for time to gather his thoughts. Doing research for novels over the course of his career, he had gained extensive knowledge on all matters paranormal. And what he didn't know he managed to make up quite nicely. He had a huge following and received countless stories of paranormal experiences from his fans.

But, he couldn't share that information with someone he barely knew. He was too protective of his identity.

So, in response to her question, he replied vaguely, "Just what I read." Tom watched her face, intrigued.

Her next question intrigued him even more.

"Do you believe in ghosts?"

Tom tilted his head and struggled to maintain an unaffected air. He thought carefully before posting an answer. In a world far, far away from Garden Ridge, he was the most famous ghost writer of them all. All of his novels centered on spirits and the supernatural. In fact, he considered himself somewhat of an expert on the subject.

But the question was did he believe in them?

He created them, sure. But did he believe?

He wasn't sure what he believed in anymore. For the two years he'd been here, he hadn't written a story, ghost or otherwise, worth giving a second glance. It had been too easy blending in with the environment. He'd never found his identity even remotely challenged. The folks in Garden Ridge didn't pry much. If anyone recognized him, they didn't let on. As long as he kept the library up and running and contributed to the local little league, they pretty much accepted him at face value. He didn't have to be anyone special.

At this moment, his identity and the subject, were not something he was willing to share. Instead, he turned the question back to her. "Do you?"

Beth wrapped her arms around herself as if she were cold. Her eyes seemed distant and troubled. After a moment, she said quietly, "I don't know."

Then, just as quickly, she seemed to come back to herself. Laughing self-consciously, she said quickly, "It's not important. Just an old house, I suppose."

Now Tom perked up, his writer's instinct on full alert. "Did something happen in the house?"

Beth stared at him silently for a moment, struggling internally, then shook her head, "No." Then, softer, "Not really."

Tom tried not to sound anxious as he asked, "Do you want to talk about it?"

Beth blinked and shook her head adamantly, as if just realizing that she had said too much. She clutched her purse and headed toward the front door. "You've been so helpful today. I'm sorry to have taken up much of your time."

Tom quelled his disappointment. He sensed that she had something on her mind. Something that could prove very important to him. Adopting a careless smile, he made a sweep of the empty room. "Time is what I have around here. Come by any time."

Beth nodded, feeling slightly ashamed that she had revealed so much to this man she barely knew. She didn't know what had come over her – she was normally a very private person. To cover her awkwardness, she smiled brightly and offered her hand, saying the first thing that came to mind, "I'm having an open house at the Laurilee Inn next Saturday. I hope you'll be able to stop by."

A flicker of interest flashed in Tom's eye as he took her hand and said warmly, "I would love to. Thank you."

His skin was warm and soft, sending a tingle coursing down her spine.

She removed her hand and slid it down by her side. Her cheeks felt flushed. She smiled to cover her nerves, but her voice still came out too rapidly as she said, "Well, great. I'll see you then." She turned toward the front door. "Good bye now."

"Bye." Tom waved and closed the door behind Beth. He stood in the doorway for a moment, his hand resting on the hard wooden door. His mind grappled furiously with something he couldn't quite grasp. Something that pertained to Beth's behavior and her interest in the paranormal. Something that pertained to the Laurilee Inn.

Tom went upstairs and stood looking out his window at the Laurilee Inn. Even though the house sparkled like new, its history surrounded it like a shroud. He could feel the secrets and stories buried deep inside. A quick surge of anticipation for the upcoming weekend surfaced. He looked forward to touring the Laurilee Inn – not to see what changes Beth had made to the exterior, but to find out what secrets lay beneath.

Something inside him whispered that Beth was the key to unlocking the writer's block that had been plaguing him for months. Tom's instincts were never wrong.

He needed Beth to trust him enough to tell him what she was hiding.

Down the street, Beth smiled as she thought of her trip to the library. She felt a connection with Tom that she couldn't quite put her finger on. It was as if she knew him already.

So, Tom Hartman had his own story and more than a few secrets. It was none of her business. She had her own secrets.

She liked him. More importantly, she felt like she could trust him.

Beth stopped and looked back over her shoulder at the library. Maybe she should have told him about the dream and the name Laurilee. Maybe he would understand.

Beth shook her head and began walking briskly away. What was she thinking? There was nothing to tell.

There was no connection between her and Tom Hartman.

Just like there was no spirit at the Laurilee Inn.

Chapter Two

"Ah, now I know it's shiny enough. I can see my reflection," Beth exclaimed as she stared down at the gleaming Heart of Pine wood in the foyer of the house.

"Excuse me?" A painter peered down at her from the scaffolding outside the window of her front room.

She had forgotten he was there, finishing up the last bit of paint on the exterior shutters on the house. With a quick wave of her hand, she said, "Never mind."

Leaving the painter to his work, Beth made one final tour of the house before its grand unveiling.

The first floor sported a renovated kitchen, a formal dining room, a library, a ballroom and a small study. The rooms were large with nine-foot ceilings. Just off the foyer, a grand staircase wound its way to the second and third floors. The steps, as well as the floors, were constructed of Heart of Pine wood, the rails long and graceful. To the rear of the kitchen, a servant's stairway also led to the upper floors.

Beth took the grand stairway, trailing her hands along the long, graceful banister.

The second floor housed five fully furnished bedrooms with new luxurious linens and curtains. Three bedrooms faced the front of the house, including a magnificent suite that opened into an ornate veranda on the second floor. Two additional bedrooms faced the courtyard to the rear of the house, one on each side of the U-shape.

Beth had booked two of the five rooms in the main house for the inaugural weekend, but she wanted the entire house to be picture perfect from the very beginning. The carriage house behind the main residence which had been converted to a garage with apartments overhead could wait until the peak summer season for final decoration, but Beth wanted the main house to look like a paradise. Forty guests had responded to her open house invitation and each one of them was a potential client.

She wanted to make just the right impression.

She had ordered linens from Atlanta in the palest of pastels; blue, green, yellow and pink. Plush towels in matching colors for the appropriate bathrooms. Crisp white guest robes for each room. Lace doilies for the dressers. Throw rugs for every room – thick and soft, round and rectangular. Sheer drapes for the windows, light and flowing to let in the morning sun. Fresh flowers with crystal vases. No detail had been overlooked.

The house smelled like lemon and fresh flowers, a crisp, clean fragrance that was pleasing to the senses.

Satisfied with the interior, Beth stepped onto the veranda. She had purchased two wicker rocking chairs with a matching table in between. A bright yellow throw blanket hung from the back of each chair. Lush hanging ferns lined the entrance to the veranda. She had done similar decorating with the second story veranda, although its use would be limited to guests in the adjoining room.

Placing her hands on the crisp white railing of the wrap-around porch, Beth surveyed the white wooden tables and chairs spread out before her on the lush front lawn. The magnificent maple trees surrounding the property shaded them perfectly. The grounds had been sprayed for pests several days ago to assure that no unwanted visitors would be infringing on the party. Fresh flowers adorned each table and the effect was refreshing and sophisticated.

The caterer stopped by and gave Beth a last minute update on the preparation of the lunch menu. She was serving crab and vegetable spring rolls, smoked duck and poblano quesadillas, smoked salmon roulades, lump crab meat and avocado salad, grilled asparagus and heart of palm wrapped with prosciutto and shrimp and artichoke skewers. For dessert, there would be strawberries dipped in chocolate, fresh fruit tarts and petite rum éclairs. Each dish had been carefully chosen and prepared to be reminiscent of a lavish southern garden party.

In one corner, under the shade of the tree and a good distance from the tables, a three-piece band practiced the soft instrumental songs that would provide the background for her luncheon. She wanted them to be part of the atmosphere, not a distraction, and they sounded lovely to her.

Satisfied that everything was in place, Beth went inside to shower and dress for the luncheon. She had left herself barely an hour to prepare.

She entered her suite on the third floor with a smile. As she had originally thought when her furniture arrived earlier in the week, she couldn't bring herself to move her bedroom pieces into the room.

Or, to be more honest, she couldn't bring herself to remove the existing pieces. Or even to move them. Somehow, they belonged exactly where they were located.

To her credit, Beth had tried to incorporate a favorite antique dressing table into the décor of the room. It was a lovely piece, low-slung and dainty with a delicate three-framed mirror. She'd had it since she was a child. In fact, it was the only piece of furniture she had taken with her to London. Still, after a full day of staring at the table and feeling the complete wrongness of it, she moved the vanity down the hall to her office.

Instead, she polished the existing furniture until it shown, keeping everything right where she had found it. She'd also left the sheer white drapes hanging in the window, electing to purchase matching linens for the four-poster bed and a stunning white hand-woven rug to cover the wood floors.

All in all, the room looked clean and feminine. Beth loved it.

The silver brush and mirror that had been left by the Lattes had been polished and sparked beneath the vanity mirror.

Beth stopped for a moment and then turned to the decorative three-drawer dresser next to her bed. Wouldn't the set look lovely on the antique lace coverlet she had placed atop the dresser yesterday?

Picking the set up gently, Beth moved them across the room, centering them carefully on the delicate lace.

"Perfect," she exclaimed, stepping back to take a look.

A chill ran along Beth's spine and she shivered for a moment. The room grew cold and Beth felt the thickness in the air. It seemed to grow heavy, pressing down on her.

She took the set and moved them back to the vanity. She couldn't explain it, but somehow she knew that was where they belonged.

Putting the brush and mirror from her mind, she gathered her toiletries and headed for the bathroom. Although the plumbing in the house was completely up to date, clearly having been renovated fairly recently, the previous owner had elected to leave the freestanding sink and bathtub. To Beth, it felt old-fashioned and luxurious and she had no intention of changing it.

Twenty minutes later, she stepped from the tub, wrapped in her soft baby-blue robe and stepped back into the bedroom.

She had laid a red sundress across the bed and put it on quickly. It was long and flowing and she loved the way it swirled across her bare ankles. There was a matching jacket in case the wind picked up, but she doubted she would need it today. She wore white sandals and very little makeup--just a touch of mascara and a dash of sheer lip-gloss. She looked young and fresh-faced. She had been blessed with clear, rosy skin and rarely wore makeup.

In contrast to her smooth clear skin; however, her long dark hair was not as easy to maintain. It was so thick and curly that using a blow dryer was a luxury she could rarely afford. Especially not today. She just didn't have the time. She'd just brush it out and tie it away from her face with a ribbon.

Frowning, Beth struggled to remember where she had stashed her hair accessories. She rummaged through her cosmetic bag and came up with nothing. Had she put them away already? With all of the distractions of the party, Beth hardly knew where her mind was half the time these days.

"This is not good," she grumbled to herself. Without something to secure it, her hair would be a mass of unruly curls in another ten minutes.

Opening the drawer to the vanity, she found the first drawer empty. The second drawer, the same. As she started to close the drawer, a flash of color caught her eye.

Beth pulled the drawer out further. Wedged into the back corner was a thin piece of fabric.

Grasping it gently with her fingers, Beth tugged at the trapped piece. It was a faded red ribbon.

Beth held the material in front of her, examining it closely.

It was faded to a lighter shade more pink than red, but obviously it had been bright once. Although the ends were slightly unraveled, it was long enough to tie into a bow.

She held it to her cheek and inexplicably felt tears prick the back of her eyes. The single ribbon touched some distant place in her heart. Some nostalgia she couldn't quite put a finger on.

Childhood.

Blinking back the threat of tears, Beth tied the ribbon around her hair. The faded color was lighter than her sundress, but she didn't care. Somehow the ribbon brought a peaceful feeling and she wanted it close to her.

She stood in a dreamlike state, admiring the ribbon in the mirror. It felt as if she were looking out through the eyes of a little girl, not really seeing her own long auburn curls and bright blue eyes, but straight dark hair and wide brown eyes. She smiled at the reflection.

The ringing of the doorbell shattered her reverie.

Beth jumped as if cannon had shot her. "Lord," she gasped, holding onto the dresser to quiet the sudden racing in her chest. Her heart hammered. She took a deep breath.

"Get a hold of yourself, girl," Beth scolded aloud. "Standing around daydreaming as if you were a lady of leisure. This won't do at all."

Beth was not aware of the strange southern drawl her voice had adopted. Still, she stood, staring at the vanity for a second longer, admiring the red ribbon, forgetting her waiting guests.

The doorbell rang again.

Beth blinked, as if coming out of a trance. She hurried down the stairs, taking the steps two at a time and skidded to a halt in front of the entrance. Taking a deep breath, she took a second to compose herself, leaving her overactive imagination behind in the bedroom.

"Well, here we go," she whispered and swung open the front door.

Tom Hartman greeted her with a smile. "I thought you might like your first guest to be someone you've at least met before."

Beth smiled back and said, "How thoughtful of you."

Tom raised an eyebrow, "Practicing your southern accent?"

Beth stared at him for a moment in confusion and then replied, "I don't know what you mean."

"Oh," Tom faltered. He was certain she had greeted him with a southern accent, but now her faint English accent held firmly in place. Shrugging, he said, "Never mind."

Then he grinned and raised an eyebrow at her. "I brought you a present."

"A present?" Beth raised her hands to her chest. "For me?"

Nodding, Tom looked over both shoulders. Not a soul in sight. Then, he took a couple of steps to the left and a couple of steps to the right, checking out the empty space around them for eavesdroppers. He stared down one of the caterers until the man blushed and scurried back inside the house.

Beth couldn't help but giggle, "Oh my."

Finally, Tom scooted back in front of her and reached inside the pocket of his tweed coat jacket. Quickly, he whipped out an object and thrust it into her hands.

Desperate to know the course of all this grand mystery, Beth dropped her gaze to the item in her hand. It was a thick black book.

Pressing her lips together, Beth turned the book to its side. Sure enough, the gold letters read: *Garden Ridge – 1800-1980*.

"Ha." She looked up at him with wide eyes. "You stole this from the library."

Tom grinned and placed a finger to his lips. "It's okay… as long as we don't tell the librarian."

"You are the librarian." But, Beth was laughing, too.

"Okay, so I'll tell everyone you checked it out." Tom's eyes danced as he watched her. He was so easy natured.

Beth felt compelled to keep up the teasing. "I don't have a library card."

Tom raised his hands in the air and shouted, "I'll get you a library card." Then he turned back to her with a softer smile. "I know how interested you are in the history of your house. I thought you might want to take some extra time to read over the book."

Beth cradled the book to her chest. "Thank you. I will enjoy reading it."

"Take as long as you like." Tom smiled and shrugged his shoulders. "The librarian is so forgetful… he probably won't miss it for ages."

"The librarian is also very sweet." Beth smiled back. "Thank you."

She stepped inside to lay the book on her parlor desk. When she returned, the next of her guests had arrived. Before she could greet them, Tom took her arm and said quietly, "You look pretty."

"Thank you." Beth felt herself blush at the kindness. She couldn't help but notice how clean cut he appeared in his tweed jacket and starched khaki pants. He looked like the boy next door, with the personality of the class clown. What an intriguing combination.

"Getting used to the place?" Tom raised his voice to include the newly arriving guests. He did, however, keep his hand resting lightly on her arm as he guided her down the path to greet her guests.

Despite herself, Beth cast a look over her shoulder towards the third story windows of the plantation house, as if expecting to see the brush and comb set floating down the white columns.

The hesitation lasted only briefly. With a quick smile, she answered everyone, "Of course. Garden Ridge is a lovely town. I'm so happy to be here."

She settled Tom in with lemonade as her guests started to arrive in force. The people of Garden Ridge were a friendly sort, pleased to meet her and anxious to share words of wisdom.

Soon enough, the local folks began sharing tales that had aged over years and years. They interrupted one another and embellished in the comfortable way that only people who have lived in the same town for a long time can understand.

Beth smiled and nodded and tried desperately to make sense of the names and places being thrown about, but she felt more of an outsider than ever. Not only was she not from Garden Ridge, she hadn't lived in the United States for over five years. Most of the people standing in her front yard, drinking tea and lemonade, hadn't wandered farther from Garden Ridge than Atlanta, four hours away. London wasn't even imaginable in their world.

Tom must have sensed her near state of panic, for suddenly he was at her side, explaining the stories he had heard too many times.

Beth smiled at him gratefully. "Am I that obvious?"

But, Tom shook his head. "You are doing wonderfully. It wasn't that long ago that I was the new kid on the block and I know how confusing these stories can be." He lowered his voice dramatically. "They exaggerate you know."

Beth laughed at his joke, but quickly returned to his first statement. "They accept you so easily, though."

Tom shrugged. "I blend in."

This time Beth really laughed. "Why do I not believe that? Every time I see you, you are the center of attention, holding court before your adoring masses. Don't think I haven't seen Mrs. Graham making eyes in your direction."

Tom rubbed his chin, nodding. "Mrs. Graham. She is a spitfire."

They both looked in the direction of the tiny, gray-haired lady, head bobbing softly as she dozed at one of the tables in the corner and burst into quiet laughter.

Beth smiled again, "You just seem like you are always having a good time."

Tom laughed, long and hard, "Life's too short not to, Ms. Willis." He pronounced her name with a thick southern accent.

She tilted her head to one side and asked, "I can't help but wonder, Mr. Hartman," she returned his southern drawl with an exaggerated English accent of her own, "if you aren't better suited to coach the high school football team than being cooped up in the library."

Tom found her soft lilt positively charming. And it suited her auburn curls and smooth clear skin to perfection. The red sundress she wore gave the impression of a certain feminine vulnerability, but he could see in her clear blue eyes that Beth Willis could take care of herself if she had to.

Now she gazed at him with one delicately curved eyebrow raised, waiting for his response. He found himself amused and intrigued by her. Not only beautiful, she was a curious one, too.

Keeping his twinkling eyes fixed on hers, he replied with a straight face, "Why, I could never give up my job at the library."

Beth frowned, pressing, "And why is that?" The time she'd visited, the place had been empty.

Tom shrugged gallantly, and replied truthfully, if not totally accurately, "Because I love books of course."

Beth harrumphed, and nodded, conceding Tom's small victory. She couldn't put her finger on it, but there was more to Tom Hartman's story. One of these days she would find out.

While the caterers set out the elaborate dessert trays, Beth gathered her guests for a quick tour of the house.

As the led them into the foyer, she explained, "The Laurilee Inn isn't just for out-of-towners, it's an escape from the every day. I hope each of you will take the opportunity to let me pamper you for a night or two."

"The living room," she explained as she lead the tour, "is a quiet place for reading or intimate conversation." The sofas were covered in dark floral damask and a fire sparkled in the mantel although the nights would soon grow too warm for fires. There was a desk for writing, equipped with stationary and stamps, a large comfortable leather chair for reading and a 1920's Victrola with relaxing records ranging from Marvin Gaye to Billie Holiday.

Through the living room was the formal dining room where dinner would be served, followed by the small library, still not quite fully stocked, but showing some lovely books that Beth had collected over the years.

"Here, in the back," Beth allowed her guests time to linger in each room before moving along, "is the parlor." She had purchased a large screen TV and stereo system to compliment the vintage pool table left over from a previous owner. The room was large and airy, the perfect setting for entertaining guests.

After a quick tour through the kitchen, Beth led the guests upstairs to the second floor. She received a chorus of "oohs" and "aahhs" as she walked through the honeymoon suite and onto the second floor balcony. Despite the dark wood of her antique furniture, she had made each room light and airy utilizing sheer flowing curtains and bright linens. The walls were painted a matte antique white and the hardwood floors were covered with thick soft area rugs.

Beth could hear several of the women discussing possible reservation dates as the group wound their way back down the stairs and out through the back door.

She concealed a pleased smile as she stopped the group in the courtyard.

The courtyard was her own little coupe de triumph. She had spent hours with a gardener designing a spectacular re-creation of some documented early 1900 gardens.

Now, she cleared her throat as her guests gathered around her. "Ladies and gentlemen, if you'll look around, I'm sure you can find the perfect spot to read the morning newspaper or sip an afternoon cocktail. Throughout the year, flowers will be in bloom beneath the shade of the maple trees."

The group clapped and inspected the lush gardens. Waiters appeared to discreetly serve dessert and lemonade as the group walked in quiet groups of two or three throughout the pebbled pathway.

The main walkway in the courtyard was bordered by boxwood. Beth had worked hard to ensure that the garden would create a visual feast that would prosper throughout the year. Springtime would be a long and lovely time full of fragrances and brightly flowered bulbs and blooming shrubs with purple and gray violets. Summer would bring roses, gardenias, jasmine and boxwood. By the end of summer, her guests would be delighted with lilies, crepe myrtle trees and other members of the amaryllis family. Groundcovers like periwinkle and edgings of boxwood would ensure that the garden plan was secure throughout the year. The walk to the carriage house was also lined with flowering bulbs and colorful ferns.

Three wrought iron benches were placed throughout the courtyard to enable the guests to truly enjoy the fresh scent of the gardens. It was a quiet, peaceful setting that Beth was certain her clients would appreciate.

As she stood sipping lemonade, Tom made his way back to her where she stood alone observing her guests. "The garden is terrific," he said as he accepted his own glass of lemonade. "How on earth did you pull it off so quickly?"

Beth raised her eyebrows and grinned. "Lots of overtime. And one very patient landscaper." She gave him a sideways glance. "Along with a little help from the local library, of course."

She had spent several hours at the library last week pouring over history books depicting 1900 plantations, copying drawings to use in her own garden. As a matter of research that was certainly in no way linked to the local librarian. If Tom just happened to stop in the room where Beth was looking over garden designs for a quick hello, well that was just circumstance.

Tom looked around with an exaggerated eye. "You came up with this great landscape from those black and white pictures we were looking at? I would have never believed it." Then he laughed, "I don't know a rose from a petunia."

Beth laughed, as well. "Flowers aren't your strong suit, Mr. Hartman?"

Tom snorted, "Hardly."

Beth tilted her head in his direction. "What is your strong suit?"

Tom stared at her for a moment with a raised eyebrow. His boyish expression was both comical and endearing. "Well, let's see," he pretended to think, tapping his index finger against the tip of his chin, "it's not art – the only picture in my house is a poster from Mardi Gras 1987. It can't be cars – I drive a Nova that puts out more exhaust than the space shuttle."

Pushing his arm lightly, Beth chided, "You're always joking around. Aren't you ever serious?"

Tom stopped and gazed at her silently. His gray eyes, typically so bright and twinkling, darkened a shade as he peered unabashedly into her eyes. He seemed to stare right through her.

His voice turned deep and smoky as he responded, "Be careful what you ask for."

Beth barely heard the words as she watched the movement of his mouth. Tom's lips, so quick to smile, suddenly seemed full and rosy and oh so kissable. Beth blushed and dropped her gaze.

Mindless of her reaction, he lifted a hand and touched a tendril of dark hair that had escaped the confines of the red ribbon. He straightened the silky curl and wrapped it around his finger. The flesh of his skin brushed against her cheek, trailing its warmth across her face. Her breath felt strained and tight. Her pulse sped and slowed along with the beating of her heart.

She leaned her head microscopically in the direction of his hand, feeling the increase in pressure against her cheek. It felt wonderful. She took a deep breath and closed her eyes.

Good lord, she wanted him to kiss her. Right here in the garden in front of forty strangers. To have him take her in his arms and press those full, ripe lips against hers. To feel the hardness of his chest, his lean waist…

"Books."

His deep, masculine voice intruded on her fantasy. Her eyes fluttered open and she asked numbly, "What?"

Tom smiled at her, the twinkle firmly reestablished. "Books are my strong suit."

Books. Beth let the word sink in for a second, bringing her back to reality. There was no kiss. No hug. No…. Beth shook away the thought.

Her cheek still felt warm from his touch, but her hair was no longer encumbered by his finger. The loose curl hung as a distraction just along the corner of her eye.

Tucking the strand behind her ear, she pursed her lips and nodded. "Books. Right. Well," she nodded again, feeling completely awkward, "that does make sense. You being the librarian and all…"

She closed her eyes and shook her head, feeling foolish. "What I meant was…"

She trailed off again. What did she mean? She had never been good at flirting – if that was indeed what had just happened. Lord, what was she thinking? Certainly, Tom was handsome and charming. To everyone. Especially strangers. She'd been aware of that fact all day long. Who was she to think she was special?

Aware of just how close she had come to making an utter fool of herself, she blurted, "I've got to go and check on the guests."

Before he could answer, she stepped away, refusing to turn her head to see if he watched her retreat.

After taking a moment to restore her composure, Beth gathered her guests for the end of the tour. Her first paying guests were due to arrive later in the afternoon and she wanted to leave enough time for the caterers to remove the tables and chairs.

As the small groups returned, there was a general buzz over the peacefulness of the garden and the lovely flowers in bloom. Beth accepted the compliments graciously and even took down several reservations for rooms over the next several weeks.

When everyone had gathered, Beth said simply, "I want to thank everyone for coming today. I hope that you will find Laurilee Inn as peaceful and relaxing as I do. I look forward to meeting you all again in the near future. Please feel free to stop by anytime. I always have lemonade."

"When can we meet your children?" A woman toward the back of the group asked.

"I'm sorry?" Beth leaned forward, thinking she hadn't heard the question properly.

"Your children?" the woman repeated clearly.

Beth shook her head and smiled, "I'm afraid it's just me here at the Laurilee Inn. I haven't any children."

The woman stepped forward, looking around the crowd. "That's odd."

"What's that?" Beth asked, completely confused.

Beth watched helplessly as the crowd leaned forward with interest to hear the woman announce loudly and with conviction, "If there are no children here – how come I can hear them laughing?"

Chapter Three

"That's impossible," Beth stated, making her way to the area in question.

The group followed, dangerously quiet. They stood, each with their head cocked slightly, listening for anything.

Beth felt the tension of the moment. Her mind worked its way back to the whispered name in her bedroom. The mysterious red ribbon. She had no explanation for those events; but, in her time here, she was certain she had never heard anything that resembled children's laughter.

After several full minutes of absolute silence, Beth said softly, "I don't hear anything. Maybe you heard the wind or a tree branches rubbing together. These old houses can make some pretty unusual noises."

The woman shrugged and nodded. "Maybe so." But, her gaze showed clearly that she didn't believe it.

Luckily, her other guests were more easily swayed. No one else had heard anything unusual and the Laurilee Inn was so lovely that by the time the last guest departed Beth had booked rooms at the Inn for the next six weeks. Several guests were even making a week of it. Beth felt sure that once the word started to spread, she would have a waiting list for the Laurilee Inn.

She couldn't wait.

"Looks like your party was a success."

She turned to find Tom walking casually through the garden in her direction. She couldn't hide her own pleased smile as she nodded. "I think you may be right."

He fell into step beside her. "You have guests arriving this weekend?"

"Actually in just a couple of hours," Beth admitted. She was on a tight schedule today. Luckily, she could already hear the sound of the caterers packing up the tables and chairs.

As they approached the rose bush where the day's excitement had taken place, Beth stopped and looked around pensively. The air around them was still and hot. A glance upward confirmed Beth's suspicion that the maple tree branches weren't blowing together as she had suggested. She honestly couldn't guess what sound had been created that would mimic a child's merriment.

She turned to Tom and asked, "What do you think that woman heard?"

Tom looked around for a moment and shrugged. "Probably the wind." Then he grinned at her. "Or, it could have been a ghost."

Beth blanched. She knew he was joking, but her palms broke out in a film of sweat. Why did he always do that? Bring up ghosts... or haunted houses? More importantly, why did she always react so strongly?

Beth swallowed the sudden lump in her throat. "You don't believe in ghosts."

Tom contradicted her by shaking his head. "I don't think I said that."

"Are you sure?"

She replayed their conversation in the library furiously in her mind. She couldn't remember the exact words. Had he said that or not? Suddenly it was very important that she know.

"Well, you do believe in ghosts?" Her voice sounded more like a frog's croak than a woman's voice.

Tom held her gaze for a long moment. Beth regarded him with such a state of near panic in her eyes that he knew he had to be very careful with his answer. He didn't want to lie to her, but he didn't want to give up his true identity. Somehow, he sensed that she saw through him, to something deeper, even if she couldn't quite put her finger on it. Exploring this conversation would only lead to more questions – questions he wasn't ready to answer just yet. One day soon, hopefully, he would be able to share his true identity. But, for now, he needed to be just Tom – the local librarian.

With a strange heaviness in his heart for keeping up the charade, Tom replied, his voice low, "No, I don't believe in ghosts."

To Tom, Beth sounded almost disappointed when she responded, "I didn't think so."

After Tom left and the caterers packed up the last of the tables and chairs, Beth took a moment to sit alone in the garden. She stared up at the back of the house.

The garden was quiet and peaceful and the house looked majestic in all of its southern splendor. She remembered the book Tom brought her and decided to go in and read for a while before her guests arrived.

In the quiet study, Beth fell back into one of the oversized leather chairs. The black book felt heavy in her hands. She rubbed her fingers over the rough, textured cover. Her mind wandered back to the day Tom had picked the book up from a stack of twenty lined on the floor of his library. How impatient she had been with his theatrics and his outrageous sense of humor. She smiled now as she thought back.

Unconsciously, she lifted the book to her face and inhaled. Maybe she was expecting the smell of his aftershave. Or the crisp wintergreen of his breath.

What she got was a nose full of dust.

Sneezing, she dropped the book back onto her lap.

"Serves you right," she mumbled, cursing herself for being so nostalgic.

She opened the book and turned to the page where the history of the Latte plantation began.

James Latte originally purchased the 100 acres of land, including a log cabin, in 1856. A year later, he built the Federal style home and called it Latte Plantation. Over the next 10 years, Mr. Latte purchased the adjoining land totaling more than 700 acres, most of which was planted in cotton.

Mr. Latte, as was the custom in those days, was a slave owner. He owned two slaves when he built the house in 1857 and, at the height of his plantation's success, owned over 30 adults and children. These slaves contributed greatly not only to the success of his plantation, but also to the smooth operations of the household.

In addition to raising cotton, the crops and livestock required to support the plantation community were actually produced on the property. James Latte also had a mill, quarry and part interest in a fishery called Penney's.

"Sounds like a busy guy," Beth whispered. She glanced at the grainy photo next to the article. She could see the plantation in the background, barely recognizable in the black and white photo. The house was new and young, its ground bare. She wondered what it was like back then, in a world so different from her own. Her eyes closed and a vision spread out before her. The photograph in her mind's eye suddenly came to life. People milled about everywhere, keeping busy. Carrying buckets of water and baskets of cotton--always careful to keep their eyes downcast. Too busy to think. There were so many jobs to do. The days passed full and hard. But, there was always food and shelter. Mr. Latte was firm, but fair; and the workers were grateful, if not satisfied. They knew others did not have it so well.

Beth's eyes popped open and she rubbed her temple, which throbbed faintly. She must have dozed off for a moment, but the images in her head seemed so real.

The ringing of the doorbell interrupted her thoughts.

"What an imagination you have," she scolded, closing the book and checking her watch. She was startled to see that two hours had passed already.

Beth walked to the door and greeted her first guests to the Laurilee Inn with a gracious smile. Mr. and Mrs. Dagnall, a newlywed couple from Texas, who had booked their room sight unseen from her web site, seemed thrilled by the appearance of the Inn.

Mrs. Dagnall, a banker in her thirties, spent a great deal of time in the formal dining room admiring the antique furniture. Her husband stopped in front of the large screen TV to watch a little of the baseball game playing soundlessly in the background.

Beth couldn't help but smile as she led the couple up the stairs to the second floor. They were obviously madly in love.

"Oh my," Mrs. Dagnall exclaimed as Beth showed them through the honeymoon suite. She, as expected, adored the 18th century four-poster bed. The thick white down comforter made the bed appear luxurious and beckoning. Even though the day was balmy, Beth had lit a fire in the second story hearth and the effect was warm and inviting. Fresh flowers adorned both nightstands and the adjoining bathroom. Beth knew that later on the couple would be pleased to find thick robes in the bathroom and a bottle of champagne cooling in a silver bucket in the sitting room.

"This is just lovely," Mrs. Dagnall breathed as she stepped onto the balcony with her husband.

"I'm glad," Beth responded, stepping out of the room. "I'll leave you two to get settled. Dinner will be in an hour."

"Thank you," Mrs. Dagnall called, but her eyes remained fixed on her new husband.

"Just give a holler if you need anything."

Beth closed the door and padded down the hall. She had a feeling that she wouldn't be hearing from the newlyweds until dinnertime.

As she descended the final stair step, the doorbell rang again.

"Mr. and Mrs. McDonald, welcome to the Laurilee Inn." Beth opened the door wide as the older couple standing on the porch smiled in welcome.

The couple passed through her tour quickly. Mr. McDonald had retired from the State Highway Department ten years previously and the couple now traveled extensively in their RV. Although they often camped, Mr. and Mrs. McDonald enjoyed the charm of the country's unique Inns whenever possible.

They seemed to Beth to be a pleasant couple, although they didn't say much as she toured them through the house. Beth had chosen a small, quaint room overlooking the courtyard for the McDonalds. They seemed pleased with the bright throw rugs and cozy patchwork quilt on the King-sized bed.

After leaving both sets of guests safely ensconced in their respective rooms, Beth ran down the back stairs to the kitchen. Rosie, her full time cook and housekeeper, had put on a pot roast with boiled new potatoes and carrots earlier in the day. Beth lifted the lid and inhaled the sweet aroma. It might not be the fanciest dinner that would ever be served at the Laurilee Inn, but it certainly smelled delicious.

As she was checking dinner, her phone rang. Beth picked up on the first ring, so as not to disturb her guests.

"Hello?" she whispered, although the guests on the second floor couldn't possibly hear her voice.

"Are they here?" Adopting her whisper, Tom's voice fluttered across the line.

"Yes." Beth smiled and looked over her shoulder. All seemed perfectly quiet.

"How are they?" He seemed to enjoy the role of co-conspirator.

"Well," Beth's smile grew, "the McDonalds are self-proclaimed experts on bed and breakfast inns, so it would seem the jury is out regarding the Laurilee Inn. I'm sure Rosie's pot roast will sway them. It smells delicious."

"Pot roast, that sounds good," Tom commented. "That should definitely do the trick."

Beth said seriously, "They seem like really nice people. I gave them the room overlooking the courtyard. If they leave the windows open tonight, they'll be able to smell the jasmine as they sleep."

"That sounds lovely. How about the other couple?"

"Ah, the Dagnalls..." Beth drew out the name and looked over her shoulder again. She'd certainly hate to be caught gossiping. "Well, the Dagnalls just got married today, so I don't imagine jasmine is exactly what they have on their minds. I put them in the honeymoon suite with strawberries and champagne."

"Perfect thinking." Tom laughed. "You're a natural."

On her end of the phone, Beth flushed at the compliment. It was exactly what she needed to hear in the midst of the craziness of the day. Her voice dropped a notch as she replied warmly, "Thank you."

"You're welcome," Tom answered easily and then said, "Is it almost time for dinner?"

"Actually, it is. In fact," Beth cocked her head toward the kitchen door, "I think I hear footsteps in the parlor."

"Okay, I'll call you later and see how dinner went," Tom promised.

Distracted by her duties, Beth responded breezily, "I'll look forward to it."

As she hung up the phone, she stared at it for a moment. Tom had called just to check in on her. And he was going to call her again later this evening. What did this mean? Beth didn't know. But, a small flutter in her stomach told her that she did indeed care.

After dinner, which was well received by both couples, Beth stood in the kitchen wiping dry the last of the dishes. She would have to invest in a dishwasher soon as her client list grew, but, for now, washing and drying her own dishes was sort of a refuge. It leant a small amount of peace to the hectic mealtime and gave her a chance to wind down.

She glanced at her watch. 8:30. It had been a long, full day. Suddenly, Beth felt as if she were made of concrete. Her legs ached from standing all day and her neck and jaw felt tense and stiff. The idea of climbing two flights of stairs seemed all but impossible. Beth paused in front of the parlor, looking longingly at the overstuffed sofa. What good was having such a comfortable room if she couldn't enjoy it every now and again? Maybe she'd just sit for a moment and collect her thoughts...

As she relaxed, she reminisced over the day. Fuzzy, jumbled thoughts swirled in her sleepy brain, seeming to center around Tom. He was such a caring man. Thoughtful, at the very least. Handsome, definitely. It had been nice of him to check on her earlier. He had said that he would call back. Beth closed her eyes and sighed deeply. 8:30 was pretty late for social calls. Still, it would be nice to hear his voice...

Fifteen minutes later the phone rang.

"Did I wake you?" Tom's clear voice rang loudly over the phone.

Beth struggled to add some life to her own groggy voice. "No, of course not."

Tom laughed, "I don't believe you."

Beth blinked. Her eyes fought to remain closed, cloaked in the darkness of sleep. She sighed, "I must have fallen asleep on the sofa."

Another chuckle. "Couldn't even make it to the bedroom, huh?"

She started to protest and then gave in graciously. "I swear the staircase grew in the last hour. I've never seen so many steps."

"Want me to come over and carry you?"

Yes, she almost screamed.

Instead, she laughed, "Oh, I suppose I'll manage."

"Okay, but if you ever need a lift…" He let his voice trail off, the laughter apparent.

"I know where to find you," she finished off with a sleepy laugh.

"Fair enough." He laughed a little and then said, "You get up to bed. I'll talk to you soon."

"Okay," Beth replied and then added, "Thank you, Tom."

"For what?" She could still hear the smile in his voice.

She smiled back. "For being such a good friend."

Hanging up the phone, she rose from the sofa and made her way to the rounded staircase. Her legs felt as if they were made of lead. She managed to wash her face and brush her teeth before slipping into her pajamas. The clock on her nightstand chimed 9:00 as her head hit the soft down pillow. Within minutes, she was asleep.

Beth felt as if she had just closed her eyes when the ringing of the phone woke her once more. Angered at the second such awakening in one night, her temple responded with an immediate pounding. She winced and struggled into a sitting position.

The red buzzer on her private line blinked repeatedly. A glance at the clock gave her the correct time. 10:30. Not nearly as late as she had imagined. And certainly not too late for one of her guests to be in need of her services.

Taking a deep breath, Beth answered the phone, making a supreme effort to sound fully alert. "Yes?"

"Ms. Willis? It's Flora McDonald. I'm sorry to bother you so late."

"It's no problem, Mrs. McDonald," Beth assured the woman. "What can I do for you?"

"Well," the older lady hesitated for a moment and then continued, "I was hoping that you could quiet down the children just a bit. I'm having a hard time sleeping."

Children? Beth sat up fully in bed. She frowned, but answered politely, "There are no children at the Inn, Mrs. McDonald."

"That's odd," the woman's voice took on a note of concern. "I've been hearing children's laughter for at least two hours. It sounds like it is coming from the courtyard. It's been quite distracting, actually."

The courtyard. A warning signal went off in Beth's brain and her heart began to pound loudly. Despite the chaos in her body, she managed to keep her voice light and unconcerned. "It must be the wind. Sometimes the caulking in these old windows comes loose. I'll come down and adjust the window for you."

She hung up the phone before the lady could respond.

Ten minutes later, clad in her robe, Beth yanked on the white-trimmed windowsill. She couldn't detect any looseness in the windowsill and the trees outside were unmoving in the stillness of the night. She paused and held her ear to the window. The house was perfectly silent. Still, she supposed it could have been the wind. If there had been any wind…

Forcing a smile that felt awkward and too bright, she turned back to the couple sitting on the edge of the bed. "There. That should take care of everything."

Mrs. McDonald looked anything but reassured. She glanced nervously at her husband and then turned to Beth. "Are you positive there were no children outside? I'm almost certain it was children's laughter I heard."

"It was the wind, Flora," Mr. McDonald moved to his side of the bed. "Let's go back to bed. I didn't hear a thing."

Mrs. McDonald shooed her husband. "Of course you didn't. You're as deaf as a doorknob. You'd sleep through a hurricane."

"Too bad I can't sleep through your yakking," her husband grumbled good-naturedly.

Beth cleared her throat and said, "Well, I'll leave you now. If you hear anything else, please give me a call."

Beth crossed her fingers behind her back. Please let them get through the night without any more noises. She didn't have much more ammunition in her bag of tricks.

The next morning, Beth arose tired and achy. She'd slept fitfully, subconsciously expecting to hear the shrill of the phone at any moment.

Greeting Rosie, who had already started breakfast, Beth poured a cup of coffee and glanced over the morning paper. The smell of bacon and sausage brought down the Dagnalls instantly.

"Good morning," the couple greeted easily and Beth filled their cups with steaming coffee.

"Good morning," Beth replied, smiling as the newlyweds remained hand-in-hand even as they sipped coffee. "Sleep well?"

The question came out smooth enough despite the butterflies in Beth's stomach. She didn't know if she could handle any more complaints of non-existent children.

After exchanging a brief, but knowing, glance clearly indicating that not much sleeping had gone on at all, Mrs. Dagnall pronounced, "I slept like a baby. Those down pillows are simply marvelous."

"Good." Beth sighed in relief.

The Dagnalls wolfed down breakfast and hustled off for a day of shopping before Rosie had even finished whipping up the next batch of biscuits.

As they left, Mrs. Dagnall turned to say, "Don't hold dinner for us. We'll probably be late."

Rosie made her way upstairs to begin laundering the linens for the afternoon while Beth finished the breakfast plates, smiling. The Dagnalls were so alive and full of energy that Beth felt exhausted just watching them.

In contrast, the McDonalds, coming down the stairs only a few moments later, seemed quiet and withdrawn. Mrs. McDonald had dark circles under her eyes and wore a pinched expression. Mr. McDonald acknowledged her warm greeting with a quick nod. Mrs. McDonald did not acknowledge her at all.

Beth didn't bother to ask how the couple had slept.

As Beth set plates of crisp bacon and fresh eggs on each placemat, Mr. McDonald picked up his fork and began to eat ravenously. His wife immediately cleared her throat and gave her husband a pointed look. He colored and sat down the utensil.

Beth turned from the counter, and asked, "Is everything all right?"

At that moment, she noticed the suitcases sitting in the doorway of the kitchen.

Mr. McDonald seemed suddenly very busy looking down at his plate, so she directed her quiet question to Mrs. McDonald. "Are you leaving?"

"Yes," Mrs. McDonald replied, pushing away her plate. "We'll be checking out this morning."

The woman made a motion to rise, but Beth placed a gentle hand on her shoulder. "At least eat your breakfast before you go."

Beth's pride stung at the obvious rejection of her Inn, but she didn't know what to say to make her guests want to stay. She didn't want anyone to feel dissatisfied. Mrs. McDonald paused indecisively for a moment and Beth added, "Rosie has already gone to the trouble of preparing breakfast, seems a shame to let the food go to waste." Beth nervously wiped her hands on the towel tucked into her apron.

Mr. McDonald watched his wife silently, obviously ready to take whatever action she deemed necessary. Finally, Mrs. McDonald took her seat and picked up her fork.

Beth released a sigh of relief.

Short-lived relief, it seemed. Without looking in her direction, Mrs. McDonald said sharply, "You may prepare our bill while we finish up if you'd like."

"Oh no," Beth held up a hand as if to ward off the stinging comment. Tears pricked at the back of her eyelids. She had never felt so mortified in her life. "There will be no charge." She wouldn't dream of charging a guest who had not had a pleasant experience.

Mr. McDonald looked up and caught her eye. His wrinkled blue eyes held hers as he said gently, "Go prepare a bill. I thought your Inn was lovely."

Beth couldn't reply through the lump in her throat. Instead, she fled the room and prepared a bill for half her normal nightly rate.

After the hasty retreat of the McDonalds, Beth sat in the kitchen motionless for several minutes. She let a few of the pent up tears trickle down her cheeks. Her first night as a bed and breakfast owner and she'd already run off half of her clients.

What was she going to do?

Beth stood and walked out into the courtyard. The morning air was crisp and clear with just a hint of winter that had not long since passed. The flowers rustled in the early morning breeze. The area was peaceful and quiet.

There was nothing to be afraid of.

Was there?

Chapter Four

With the Dagnalls out for the day and the McDonalds gone, Beth decided to spend the day refinishing an old rocker she had picked up at a garage sale. The large, sturdy chair would look lovely on the porch once it was stripped and painted bright white.

She spread out an old sheet on the drive in front of the carriage house and donned her sturdy latex gloves. The heavy acrid smell of the remover assaulted her nostrils as she opened the can. She looked skyward and blinked her eyes several times as they watered in protest.

The sky shone cloudless and blue. Although summer was just around the corner and the temperature during the day was rising, there was still a hint of spring left in the air. A gentle breeze carried the fragrant aroma of her garden to replace the sting of the paint stripper. She sneezed and blinked once more before returning her attention to the rocker before her.

As she lowered her gaze, a shadow from the house caught her attention. She swung her head back in that direction, blinking out the remaining water from her eyes. The back of the house rose before her, majestic in the sunlight. She inventoried the rows of windows quickly, but everything seemed in order. She felt certain she would have heard if the Dagnalls had cut short their shopping expedition. The driveway leading to the front gate was empty. The air around her was still and quiet.

Shrugging the shadow from her mind, she turned back to the rocker.

Two hours later, as the rocker gleamed with its first coat of paint, Beth sat up and stretched her back. She felt an inner peace that had been missing for too long. How much she had changed in the past year. Leaving London for the sleepy town of Garden Ridge, it seemed impossible almost that she would be satisfied away from the bustle of the city. But, there was much to love about her new home.

Time. Typical for small towns, Garden Ridge moved at a slow, relaxed pace. Time took on a different context. There was no meeting to rush to. No urgent appointments to attend.

Freedom. No one was looking for her. Or awaiting a decision, an answer, a request.

It felt good.

Beth closed her eyes briefly, savoring this moment of peace and contentment. She opened her eyes and surveyed the garden before her, blossoming in the spring air. Its lusty fragrance filled the yard with sweetness. The house towered, glorious and clean, three stories behind it. She sought the window of her third floor room. Her private retreat.

Eyes narrowing, Beth sat up. There it was again. In the window of her office. That shadow.

She stood and walked forward several steps, staring intently, expecting the shadow to disappear under her scrutiny.

But, the dark shape didn't move. And Beth's heart stopped for a moment as she looked closer at the window of the suite in which she worked.

It wasn't a shadow.

It was a figure.

And it was staring back at her.

Finding her feet, Beth took off through the garden and into the back of the house. She climbed the stairs two at a time, hanging onto the railing for dear life.

She spun into her office, throwing open the door. She skidded to a stop. The room was freezing.

Grabbing her sweater from the chair and throwing it over her shoulders, Beth quickly scanned the room. It was empty. She was certain. However, the air felt heavy. Pregnant with the presence of someone, or something.

Beth walked to the window and looked out. From this vantage point, she could see the rocking chair sitting where she left it near the carriage house. She reached out tentatively and touched the glass. It was warm.

"Rosie," she called, "are you up here?"

Even as she said the words, she knew there would be no answer. Rosie's job was to make up the guest rooms. She had no business on the third floor and would never come up here without talking to Beth first.

Beth turned back and surveyed the room. Already, the temperature had warmed to a comfortable degree.

She made a cursory inventory of the room. Nothing seemed out of place. Her desk remained untouched. No fingerprints on the window.

She crossed the hallway into her bedroom, glancing about pensively. She shivered, more out of nerves than any chill in the air, but put the sweater on regardless, wrapping it tightly around her. Again, everything seemed in order. Her bed remained freshly made, it's quilt tucked tightly into the bed frame. The things on her nightstand…

Shaking her head, she moved away from the dresser and then suddenly froze. In her mind's eye, she pictured the nightstand. Something was awry. Taking a slow breath, she turned back around.

Yes. She took a step forward. Her family Bible stood open on the nightstand. She kept it close for sentimental reasons, but did not read from it regularly.

Hand shaking, she approached the book and turned it to face her.

It was open to the book of Psalms. And a page was missing, leaving a jagged edge in the delicate book.

Beth felt a distinct pressure behind her, as if someone were staring intently at her back. The hairs on her neck rose in protest.

"Who's here," she shouted in the empty room, feeling foolish. The room was obviously empty.

Taking deep breaths to quiet her pounding heart, she ran through the rest of her suite. As expected, she found nothing out of the ordinary.

She returned to the Bible, feeling somewhat violated. That book had belonged to her parents. It was one of the few memories she held of her past. How dare someone, or something, invade her privacy like that.

She grabbed the book and held it to her chest.

"Stay out of my room," she warned aloud to nothing in particular, "and stay away from my things."

Beth ran down the stairs, clutching the Bible. Not knowing where else to turn, she decided to head to the library.

She entered the old house in a flurry, slamming the door behind her. Presently, Tom appeared from the back room.

"Beth." He seemed pleased to see her.

Beth, on the other hand, had a one-track mind. "I need to see a Bible."

Tom raised an eyebrow at her slightly hysterical tone, but did not comment. Instead, he turned and led her to a room off what used to be the parlor. No theatrics this time. He pulled a large leather-bound book from the shelf and handed it to her.

She took the Bible and sat down at a large wood table nearby. She placed the two books side by side; her Bible open to the page in question. Feeling her heart pound in her chest, Beth opened the book and turned to the book of Psalms. She quickly turned to the page that had been torn from her book. Because of the difference in print size, she double checked, verifying the exact Psalm missing.

Beth read the passage on the page before her.

Praise the LORD! Praise, O servants of the LORD, praise the name of the LORD!

Blessed be the name of the LORD from this time forth and for evermore!

From the rising of the sun to its setting the name of the LORD is to be praised!

The LORD is high above all nations, and his glory above the heavens!

Who is like the LORD our GOD who is seated on high,

Who looks far down upon the heavens and earth!

He raised the poor from the dust, and lifts the needy from the ash heap,

To make them sit with princes, with princes of his people.

He gives the barren woman a home, making her the joyous mother of children.

Praise the LORD.

"Praise the LORD." The words rolled easily from Beth's tongue as if she'd said them a million times. The passage felt so familiar, although she didn't think she'd heard it before.

"Is everything okay?" She could hear the concern in Tom's voice as he stood behind her.

Beth could only shake her head, rubbing her hand across her forehead. "A page is missing from my Bible. I wanted to see what it was."

"What happened to it?" Tom cocked his head to one side, waiting.

"I don't know," Beth replied. She hadn't opened the Bible in years. That page could have been missing for ages.

She shivered and instinctively thrust her hands into the pockets of her sweater.

A thin crumbling sound pounded in her ears. Her blood ran cold. Removing the ball from her pocket, her very breath shook. She didn't even have to look. She knew what it was.

Still, as if guided by an unseen force, she straightened the delicate paper, smoothing its fragile edges. She ran her fingers along the torn edge. She placed it, carefully, on the open bible. It fit perfectly against the jagged edge of the book. She pushed the book away as if scalded, sending the Bible skittering across the table.

Tom retrieved it and held it out to her, serious questions in his eyes. "Is everything okay?"

She shook her head and stood up, backing away. She croaked, in a voice raspy with emotion, "I did it. I tore the page out."

"Okay," Tom tried to be rational. He could sense the panic in her eyes, but didn't understand it. "Maybe it wasn't your favorite passage."

She didn't laugh at his weak attempt at humor. Instead her eyes took on a faraway look. "Actually, I loved that passage. It gave me comfort." She toyed with her hair, all the while looking out at something Tom clearly couldn't see.

Tom frowned. Her voice sounded different, softer somehow and her mannerisms were girlish almost. Then he noticed how very pale she was and that spurred him into action.

"Beth," he called, a little loudly, touching her shoulder. "Are you okay?"

Beth blinked, stared at him blankly for a split second and then nodded. "Of course. I'm fine." She took the book from his outstretched hand and tucked it under her arm, not looking at it again. "I have the morning off and I really want to do some more research about the town. That's why I came here. This Bible thing," she waved it off, "was just something I was curious about."

Her words came out too fast and she clamped her mouth shut. She knew she couldn't hide the emotion in her face. How had the missing page ended up in her sweater? Had someone put it there? Or had she torn the page out herself and didn't remember? Beth searched her memory, but save for setting the Bible on her nightstand when she unpacked her things, she knew she hadn't touched the book.

And the passage... It felt so familiar to her, almost as if she knew it by heart. But, she didn't know it. She'd never heard it before.

Tom watched the emotions move across Beth's face. She still seemed flustered, but the color was back in her cheeks and she appeared more in control, even though she would not meet his eyes. "Beth..." he started, clearly concerned about her.

She cut him off, raising a hand that shook slightly. "Tom, I'm fine. Really." She nodded to emphasize her point, and her eyes pleaded with him to let the subject drop.

He watched for a long moment and then shrugged easily. "I was just going to say that I was about to head to the diner for lunch. Care to join me?"

Beth's stomach grumbled and she was forced to laugh. She hadn't eaten since breakfast.

Since she wasn't ready to face the silent, empty house, she readily agreed.

They walked the short distance to the diner in comfortable silence, enjoying the sunny day.

Once inside, they chose a red vinyl booth in the corner. The diner was quiet and Beth felt herself finally start to relax under the easy conversation with Tom

After they placed their orders, Tom leaned back and folded his hands behind his head. "So, how's business?"

"The McDonalds checked out this morning," Beth admitted quietly.

"Really? The older couple?" Tom frowned in surprise. "What happened? Did they get lonely for the RV?"

Beth shook her head. "Apparently, Mrs. McDonald had trouble sleeping." She didn't elaborate.

Tom pursed his lips. "In those beds of yours? Must be an insomniac or something."

Beth just nodded. Or something.

"I bet you were disappointed," he commented lightly.

Beth nodded again. "A little."

"Well, it's just the first week. Things will pick up. How about the newlyweds?"

This time Beth smiled. "Happy as clams."

Tom laughed, "You have that going for you."

Beth laughed as well. He always knew just how to put things in perspective.

Their orders arrived and, for a while, they ate in comfortable silence. Then Tom, munching on a French fry, asked, "Do you miss England?"

She knew he was just making conversation, but the subject brought a flush to Beth's cheeks. She tried to keep her answer on safe grounds. "Some things I miss--like the antique gallery where I worked. I thought I would miss the hustle and bustle of the city, but I really don't. I find the peace and quiet of a small town surprisingly refreshing."

"You know your accent grows more pronounced when you speak of England."

Beth laughed. "I worked so hard on it when I arrived, I'm not surprised it has lingered. I wanted to sound perfectly British even though I was born and raised in Atlanta." She blushed, thinking back. "Silly, isn't it?"

"Not so," Tom corrected. "It sounds like you were set on adopting a new identity."

It was a very perceptive comment and Beth replied without stopping to check herself, "More like running from an old one."

Tom raised an eyebrow. Beth struggled to find a suitable explanation for her comment. After a moment, she said, "You might find this hard to believe, but I was fairly conservative growing up."

Tom feigned a look of shock. "You? Conservative? Never."

Beth allowed a small laugh to escape. "Well, I was. The classic poor little rich girl. I had a nanny and a butler, but no real friends." She sighed wistfully. "How I always wanted friends." She trailed off, looking sad.

"Anyway, when I moved to England, I desperately wanted to be a starving artist, so I threw away all of my designer clothes and ran around in a smock and beret. It seemed very glamorous at the time."

Tom watched her closely. She felt he could really see through all of the hurt she kept inside. She felt exposed and vulnerable. But, he was so gentle and kind. He asked, "So, were you?"

She was momentarily caught off guard and asked, frowning, "Was I what?"

"A starving artist," he prompted.

"Oh," she laughed thinking back, and then shook her head. "No. I worked in an antique store and ate quite well, thank you. What about you?" She smiled coyly. "Any dreams of being a starving artist for you?"

Tom could have kicked himself. He had led himself right into that trap. If she only knew that he had indeed been a starving artist for years before his first book was published. He was afraid if he said anything, he would blow his cover and he wasn't ready to do that just yet. Adopting a smile, he spread his arms. "What you see is what you get."

"Somehow I doubt that," Beth replied evenly and then changed the subject. "Have you always been a librarian?"

Tom shook his head. "Before that, I was the star quarterback for the Highland Grove Daredevils."

Beth raised her eyebrows, "I didn't know you were a local boy." Highland Grove was less than two hours down the coastline from Garden Ridge. "Do you still have family there?"

"No." Tom grew quiet. "My parents are dead. I'm an only child."

Beth felt her heart catch for a second. Then she placed her hand over his and said softly, "My parents died, too."

Tom's eyes widened. "I'm sorry." His words sounded genuine and sympathetic. "What happened? If you don't mind my asking," he added in a hurry.

Her smile was soft and sad. "They died in a car accident just after my eighteenth birthday." She sighed. "I suppose I should be grateful that I had a family for as long as I did, but all I remember is feeling completely lost and alone."

"Didn't you have relatives?"

Beth shook her head. "No. I was an only child, too." Her voice cracked a little. "I had no one."

"Is that why you went to England?"

Beth nodded, being honest with him. "I couldn't take the loneliness. Europe seemed like a great place to escape." She closed her eyes for a moment, feeling ashamed of her weakness. She had fled to Europe to escape her parents' death and then run here to escape Europe. Would she ever stop running?

With an effort, she pushed the thought aside, and said more lightly, "Again, I'm fortunate that my family was well off. I lived for a year off the trust fund my parents left me and got my business certificate through correspondence school."

"But you were alone," Tom stated, covering her hand with his own.

His concern touched her and, for the first time in a long time, Beth felt comfortable sharing information about her life. She had kept her emotions bottled up for so long, the release felt almost liberating.

To answer his question, she smiled. "Eventually, I took a job in a local antique gallery to help pass the time. I found myself intrigued by the intricate details of the elaborate pieces the gallery carried. The owner was an ancient Englishman who was more than willing to share his knowledge with me. I absorbed it like a sponge. It was the first sign that I still had some life in me." She trailed off for a moment and then answered Tom's original question. "And then I met Jean-Pierre and I wasn't alone anymore."

"Jean-Pierre?" Tom's soft voice barely cut through her memories.

"He was ten years older than me. He walked into the antique shop before my twentieth birthday, all designer suits and dark intense eyes. He stared right through me, undressing me with his eyes." She laughed, a little embarrassed. "I know that sounds ridiculous, but that is exactly what happened. And, from that moment on, for the next five years, I belonged to him."

"Sounds serious," Tom commented.

Beth pulled out of her reverie and shook her head. "Intense, yes. Serious, never. Jean-Pierre was so strong and so brooding. I was overwhelmed by his intensity and followed his lead without question. He seemed to know so much and was so confident. I never thought to question his motives. I was always just a little surprised that I caught his attention and managed to hold on to it for five years."

It was the most honest statement Beth had ever made about her relationship with Jean-Pierre and it still stung to hear the words come from her lips.

"What happened?" Tom was watching her closely, noting the changes in her expression.

The old pain flared up and Beth choked on her next words. "He was married." She shook her head helplessly. "I never suspected a thing. I was so stupid."

"Don't say that." Tom practically spat out the words. "He took advantage of you. Shame on him." He grasped her hands and looked at her with passion flaring in his eyes. "That man did not deserve your love."

"Thank you, Tom," Beth whispered, looking deep into those gray eyes. His hands felt warm and strong as they covered hers and she felt safe and protected.

Beth could see how genuine and passionate Tom felt about the subject. He sounded like someone who would never take advantage of another person. He cared much too deeply. She knew that was a rare and special trait and it touched her.

At the same time, her own scars ran too deep. The threat of another betrayal, any betrayal, sent her mind into a tailspin. She couldn't handle that kind of rejection again. Her heart might break for good the next time.

Aware that she was treading on rocky ground, Beth removed her hands from his and changed the subject abruptly. "So, enough about me. What about you? Didn't like being a small town boy?"

Tom watched her silently for a moment, speaking volumes with his eyes. He seemed to sense that she wasn't ready to take the conversation further and allowed her to escape. But, she knew for certain that the subject would come up again.

He shrugged. "Ironic, isn't it? I left Highland Grove right out of high school. Off to claim my fortune and fame, I suppose. I never wanted to look back."

"But, you did," Beth pointed out.

"Yeah, here I am." Tom grinned ruefully. "It's funny how life takes you places you never thought you would go."

"Yes, it is," Beth echoed, thinking how wise Tom was. She had a strong feeling that his life wasn't nearly as simple as he liked people to believe. He had too much knowledge. Too much understanding.

She tried to press him, bringing the subject back to her curiosity. "So, you went from high school jock to meek librarian in one straight jump?"

"Not so straight," Tom said. "I was a waiter, a lifeguard and a car wash attendant in between." He rattled off a list of odd jobs he had held while waiting to get his first book published.

Beth whistled, "Impressive." Then she added with a touch of gentle sarcasm, "I can see where that would lead right to the library."

Tom raised a sardonic eyebrow. He really hated being dishonest. She was such a genuine person. He added seriously, "I've always loved books. It's where I fit in. Besides," he threw his hands out wide. "I like being the librarian in Garden Ridge. Do you know when the last time someone failed to pay a late fee on an overdue book? 1963."

"Would that be the same year the library actually got a new book?" Beth teased.

"Ouch." Tom held his hand over his heart. "That hurt."

But, he was smiling as he took care of the check.

After lunch, the two walked aimlessly through the town. There was easiness about Tom that eased Beth's normal tension. She was gun shy around men, but Tom didn't pressure her. Even when he touched her arm to get her attention, his touch was warm and reassuring, not threatening.

She followed his gaze to a lake where a family of ducks paddled merrily along the water's edge. On the other side of the lake, a couple played fetch with a magnificent golden retriever, enjoying the coolness of the day. Beth and Tom watched in silence for several moments as the dog flew across the grass in pursuit of a bright orange plastic stick. Even when his master overthrew the lawn and the stick landed in the water, the dog didn't miss a beat. Airborne, golden hair flying behind him, the dog leapt in the water and snatched his toy, returning it, tail wagging in pride, to his master.

"What a great life." Tom grinned as he watched the dog's antics.

Beth turned to face him. What a great smile he had. His face lit up when he laughed, which was often, but, his smile alone was simply devastating. It softened his face and gave him a dreamy look in contrast to the deep lines of his jaw. She had the urge to place her palm along the side of his cheek.

As if she'd spoken her errant thought aloud, Beth blushed and stepped away from Tom. "I'd really better get back."

"Are you sure?" Tom turned towards her. His eyes were bright and friendly, as if he didn't have a care in the world.

Beth held his gaze for a moment and then, afraid she might lose herself in it, she blinked and nodded. "Yes, the Dagnalls might be back and I have to help Rosie get dinner ready."

"Okay." Tom nodded agreeably. He was always agreeable.

They walked together back to the library. Beth could not help but smile to herself as she watched Tom go back inside. They had been gone for over an hour and old Mrs. Petty was sitting on the front porch, calm as could be, when they arrived. Tom hadn't made any excuses as he kissed the old woman on the cheek and led her inside. Nor had Mrs. Petty asked for any. It was apparently not a problem for the library to close for several hours in the middle of the day in Garden Ridge. Of course, there weren't many problems in general in Garden Ridge.

Except for phantom cries in the night and missing book pages. But, that only seemed to happen at the Laurilee Inn.

Beth sighed and headed home.

The Dagnalls arrived late in the afternoon, arms laden with bags.

"There is the cutest little antique shop over on Main Street," Mrs. Dagnall gushed. "I found an authentic Eastlake desk. It's simply fabulous."

Beth was also partial to the Eastlake design and the two women chatted compatibly about antiques while Beth put the finishing touches on dinner. Rosie had put lasagna in the oven almost an hour ago and all Beth had to do was throw together the salad and heat up breadsticks to compliment the meal.

The doorbell rang just as Mr. and Mrs. Dagnall retired upstairs to change for dinner.

Wiping her hands on her apron, Beth opened the front door. A young couple, strikingly similar in appearance to the Dagnalls, greeted her.

The woman's eyes were red and puffy and she lowered her head as soon as Beth appeared in the doorway. The man next to her placed his arm around her shoulders in comfort while saying to Beth, "We're awfully sorry to barge in like this, but we saw your sign from the road. Our car broke down on the Interstate. We brought it to the mechanic in town, but," he took a deep breath, "it seems that it's going to take a day or two to order the parts."

An audible sob escaped the woman's throat and the man shifted uncomfortably and continued in a rush. "Well, it's our honeymoon and we were on our way to Savannah, but," he raised his hands helplessly, "now, it seems we're in somewhat of a bind."

The woman's shoulders heaved as she struggled to maintain her composure. Clearing his throat, the man finished off, lowering his head in defeat even as he asked, "I'm sure you are probably full at this late hour, but maybe you could recommend someplace for us to stay...."

"Actually," Beth smiled, "I just had an unexpected cancellation this morning." With the departure of the McDonalds, she had been concerned that the momentum of her Inn would slow down. Another set of guests would really help her out.

Both heads snapped up. The woman's eyes lit up. "Really?" She looked at her new husband hopefully. They, like the Dagnalls, seemed young and madly in love.

Beth's smile grew as she stepped out of the doorway. "Please come in. I'm Beth Willis, the owner of the Laurilee Inn."

The couple introduced themselves as the Wrights and Beth led them up the grand staircase to the second floor, explaining as she walked, "I'm afraid the honeymoon suite is already booked, but I have another lovely room in mind."

"We're just happy to be here," Mr. Wright offered, even as his wife took hold of the surroundings. "We can't thank you enough for taking us in."

"Nonsense." Beth raised her hand, dismissing the thanks. "I'm happy to have you both."

She stopped in front of the room next to the Dagnalls; a small, but just as cozy, version of the honeymoon suite with its own fireplace and soft down comforter. Beth went to the window and pulled open the drapes. It was no coincidence that this room faced the front of the house. It may be a bunch of nonsense, but Beth wasn't taking any chances that this couple might hear phantom noises in the courtyard.

"Oh, this room is wonderful." Mrs. Wright ran her hands over the mahogany dresser. Her eyes lit up as she looked at her husband and Beth was very glad she had been able to help the young couple.

"Well," she moved to the door, "you made it just in time for dinner, if you're hungry. I expect the Dagnalls will be down any moment. They are newlyweds as well. I think you will get along just fine."

Truer words had never been spoken. The Dagnalls and the Wrights hit it off famously. It seemed that they had many common interests and, before dinner was through, the Wrights had called Savannah to cancel the remainder of their reservations and had extended their stay at the Laurilee Inn through the end of the week. Beth couldn't have been happier.

Leaving her guests sipping an after-dinner brandy in front of the fire in the living room, Beth retired to her own suite. She resisted the urge to call Tom and tell him the good news. She had been raised that it wasn't proper for girls to call boys and somehow the philosophy stuck.

Still, she couldn't help picturing his laughing gray eyes as he told a funny story at lunch. He always seemed to have an anecdote or humorous outlook for every situation. Just thinking about him brought a smile to her face. He was so different from Jean-Pierre. Jean-Pierre had been brooding and dark. Beth had found herself constantly on guard when Jean-Pierre was around. His moods changed abruptly. And, sometimes, he could be very cruel.

In stark contrast, Tom was easy to be with. She felt no pressure from Tom. He seemed like a man who could find happiness in any situation. In return, he spread his good cheer to others. While picking up groceries the other day, she had overheard two ladies talking about what a wonderful little league coach Tom was. He was involved in so much, yet he always had time to listen.

The last picture in her mind before falling asleep was Tom.

A half mile away, Tom stood looking out the window at the darkened streets below. Behind him, the dull glow of the computer cast an eerie light over the room. The screen was blank after the last hours' worth of work had been abruptly erased. Tom's mind swirled with frustration. He needed something to boost his imagination. An idea to jumpstart his creative juices. And then his natural instincts would take over. But, his mind refused to cooperate.

In the distance, the peak of the Laurilee Inn caught his eye. He thought of Beth inside, asleep. His heart ached for a moment. She thought he was something that he was not. With a sigh from his soul, Tom turned back to his computer.

Chapter Five

The next month passed with no further incident at the Laurilee Inn. Beth had a steady stream of guests with no re-occurrences of any unusual noises in the middle of the night. She'd had lunch with Tom several times and every time found him easier to talk to. They laughed a lot and Beth smiled when she thought of him.

Tonight they were having dinner. She currently had three couples in the Inn, but Rosie had left a huge pot of chili on the stove and tonight's dinner would be self-serve for the guests. They didn't mind. Each couple had a full day of events planned and supper would be casual for all of them.

Beth stood in her closet, looking over her sparse wardrobe. The fanciest restaurant in Garden Ridge was the diner and jeans would be perfectly acceptable. But, she wanted to make a good impression on Tom. He had been such a good friend to her.

She finally decided on a red wrap-around skirt with a white tailored shirt and sandals. The bright skirt heightened the red highlights in her hair and she tied it back with the faded red ribbon she had found in her vanity, leaving a few loose curls around her face. In the last several weeks, Beth had found herself reaching for the ribbon more and more frequently. The ribbon gave her a sense of security that she could not logically explain.

She leaned forward and studied her face in the mirror. A spattering of brown freckles danced along the ridge of her nose. She knew that in a matter of months, as the weather grew warmer, those freckles would become even more apparent.

She ran a hand over the bridge of her nose. Somewhere in the recess of her memory came the shadow of a different complexion. One that was smooth and the color of coffee with cream.

Her hand trailed along her cheekbone until she reached a tendril of dark hair curled around her ear. She touched the soft strand, feeling its silkiness. In her mind, she felt a strand of thick, course hair, still long, but never allowed to hang loose.

She blinked in the mirror. Were those loose hairs around her face? How had that happened? Her eyes widened as she grasped the stray tendrils, struggling to push them back into the ponytail. Then she stopped, even further mortified, and leaned forward until her face almost touched the mirror. Was that rouge on her cheeks and her lips? She gasped in horror, slapping at her cheeks.

"Oh, Lordy, Lordy…" she moaned, rushing to the bathroom, "if he sees me like this…"

The unfamiliar high pitched wail trailed off as she splashed water on her face, rubbing off the offensive rouge and lipstick. Then, she pulled down the loose ponytail and twisted her hair into a severe knot at the back of her neck. The discarded ribbon fluttered to the ground.

Finally, she breathed a sigh of relief. "There now," she murmured in her thick southern accent. "Everything is fine now."

Smoothing the front of her skirt, Beth went back into the bedroom.

She was sitting on the bed, reading, when the doorbell rang thirty minutes later.

She glanced at the clock on the nightstand. "Right on time," she said, her light British accent carrying a snappy lilt.

As she passed by the dresser, she glanced at her reflection and then stopped short.

"What…" she breathed aloud as she caught site of her reflection.

Turning slowly, she stared at the mirror in disbelief. Her skin, rubbed free of makeup, shone slightly red still from the vigorous rubbing. Beth reached up behind her head to feel the knot twisted so tightly she could feel the hair pulling from her scalp.

Her frown deepened as she looked around the room in confusion. What had she done? She made her way to the bathroom almost in a daze. Inside, she spotted the red ribbon lying on the floor. In the sink, a washcloth bore the remains of her painstakingly applied makeup. She reached down and picked up the ribbon, shaking her head in disbelief. Obviously, she had changed her appearance.

What else had she changed? She looked down and breathed a sigh of relief. At least her clothes were the same. But, what had happened over the last half hour? Had she had some sort of anxiety attack? Some sort of black out? It didn't make any sense.

The doorbell rang again.

Glancing around quickly, Beth didn't have time to think. She freed her hair from the knot and let it fly loose in a mass of curls. She lay the ribbon down gently and grabbed a tube of lipstick from the counter. It would have to do.

Beth threw open the front door just as Tom was reaching for the doorbell for the third time.

"I'm sorry," Beth cried breathlessly. "I didn't hear the bell."

"It's okay." Tom smiled and held out a single daisy. His expression was so pure and genuine that Beth's own heart skipped a beat.

She took the flower and held it to her cheek. "That's so sweet. It looks just like the ones in my garden."

Tom blushed.

Raising her eyebrows, she removed the flower and gave it a closer look. He coughed and looked guilty, but not really. He smiled beguilingly. "It's the thought that counts, right?"

"Absolutely," Beth agreed. Her garden wouldn't miss one flower and it was such a sweet gesture.

"Shall we go?" Tom asked, offering his arm.

As Beth linked her arm through Tom's, any thoughts of her earlier episode escaped her mind completely.

After dinner, Tom surprised her by asking if she wanted to go to the movies.

Beth frowned, "I didn't know Garden Ridge had a theater."

"It doesn't." Tom grinned. "We'd have to go to Golden Grove."

Golden Grove was 25 miles away.

Beth grinned, feeling like a naughty teenager. "Oh, yes, let's do it."

As they drove along the narrow, two-lane highway, Tom found an oldies station and they listened comfortably, chatting idly about the weather and national politics. Tom seemed to know something about every subject as he switched easily from politics to Shakespeare to baseball season. Beth considered herself an intellectual and certainly kept abreast of current events, but she was still impressed with his depth and absolute command of the conversation. The time passed in a whirlwind of interesting stories.

When they turned off the highway onto a narrow dirt road, Beth leaned forward with curiosity. Ahead of them loomed a massive white movie screen. A red neon marquee announced the Golden Grove Drive Inn.

"A drive in?" Beth shook her head in amazement. "I thought they had become extinct decades ago."

"This may be the last one," Tom deadpanned. "If we're lucky, the movie will even be one of those newfangled talking pictures."

"Talking pictures, you say?" Beth turned to him, eyes wide, playing along. "What will they think of next?"

The movie turned out to be a relatively current action flick that neither one had seen, but both enjoyed tremendously.

About halfway through the movie, Tom leaned over and whispered with a smile in his voice, "You know, there is one big advantage to having a vintage car."

Vintage was an interesting term for the battered green Chevy Nova they were sitting in, but, Beth took the bait, turning her head to look at him. "What's that?"

He patted the green vinyl space between them. "No bucket seats."

She let the statement sink in for a moment before realizing that it was in invitation for her to scoot closer to him. She took a deep breath. If she did that, she'd certainly be able to smell the manly scent of his aftershave. And, whenever he spoke, she'd surely be able to feel the warmth of his breath against her skin. And the soft denim of his blue jeans might rub against her bare skin if he stretched out his legs. Being that close to Tom was dangerous and Beth felt her heart race as she thought of it.

When she met his gaze, it was almost as if he were reading her thoughts. His mouth curved in a "come and get me" grin and his eyes twinkled with what felt like a challenge. She decided to accept that challenge by saying in a saucier voice that camouflaged her inner insecurity, "I thought you'd never ask," and then inched sideways across the seat until they were side by side.

"Thanks." Tom gave her another smile and turned back to the movie.

"Sure," she replied, feeling a little awkward. Now that she was here, what was she supposed to do? As usual, Tom made it easy for her. He slipped his arm around her shoulders, drawing her into the comfortable circle of his arm.

The rest of the movie passed in a blur. Beth tried to focus on the fast-paced action showing on the screen, but all she could think about was Tom's hand resting lightly on her shoulder. The light pressure of his fingers seared through her thin shirt and scorched her skin. The smell of his aftershave teased her nostrils, driving her crazy. Each time he shifted positions, butterflies raced through her stomach. She fought the urge to turn and watch the profile of his strong, sturdy jaw or to reach up and lace her fingers through his.

Too soon, the movie ended.

As the credits rolled, Tom leaned forward and started the engine. With his arm removed from her shoulder, Beth felt cold and alone.

She started to move back to her side of the car, but as soon as she shifted her body weight his arm snaked back around her and pulled her close. She glanced up at him, feeling whole again as her body meshed against his. He smiled and dipped his head to drop a feather kiss on the tip of her nose.

No words were spoken and Beth didn't want the moment to end. Instead, she dropped her head onto Tom's shoulder as they drove along the narrow road towards Garden Ridge. The darkness outside, coupled with the soft music playing in the background, lulled Beth into a peaceful dream state. Her eyelids grew heavy as she watched the dark outline of the trees pass by in a shadowy blur.

She spoke in a dreamy voice, "Isn't it sad that so many of the plantation homes were destroyed over the years? Remember when they used to stretch for acres and acres – all the way to the ocean?"

Tom's voice reached her ears from far away. "I think that's just one of the consequences of industrialization--cities grew to support the land and the land shrunk to support the cities."

"But, I remember when a plantation could take care of itself. Why we had our own smokehouse and blacksmith right on the land. And a saw mill and a cotton press, too. We raised crops and livestock to support the entire plantation, including all of the educated people that lived in the main house, but still we supported them all right..."

"Beth..."

Beth lifted her head from Tom's shoulder and looked up at him. He looked very upset and his voice had been raised.

She frowned at him. "What's the matter?"

He frowned back. "You said we."

Beth was confused. She hadn't said anything. "What do you mean?"

He spoke slowly and clearly, as if to a child, "You said WE had our own smokehouse and blacksmith." He raised an eyebrow expectantly.

"I did?" Beth felt a knot in her chest. She searched her memory, but still couldn't remember any sort of conversation about blacksmiths. She remembered watching the trees go by and then Tom shouting her name, but nothing in between. She must have been half asleep.

"Yes," Tom practically shouted. "You were talking about life on the plantation and you kept saying we."

She shrugged now, trying to cover her lapse in memory. She blurted out the only thing that made sense. "I was talking about the Latte's, of course."

Tom nodded skeptically. "Okay, but, you were talking with a Southern accent."

Beth raised a hand to her forehead, where she was starting to get a headache. Oh, Lord, what next? She wasn't about to admit that she didn't remember an entire conversation. Issuing a forced laugh, she said, "You're not the only one allowed to joke. I was fooling with you."

Tom stared at her for another moment and then laughed with only the slightest lingering of doubt. "You should go into impressions. That accent was very good."

Beth exhaled the breath she had been holding and said a silent prayer of thanks. That had been a close call.

When they pulled up in front of the Laurilee Inn, Beth sighed. She didn't want the evening to end.

Always the gentleman, Tom walked her to the door. Standing on the porch, Beth looked at Tom and said softly, "I had a lovely time tonight. Thank you."

"I'm glad you had fun," he whispered, his voice low and sexy in the stillness of the night.

He placed his hand along the side of her cheek and gently guided her toward him. His lips were soft against hers. The kiss was gentle and intimate, with promises of good things to come. He pulled away too soon, leaving Beth breathless and wanting more.

"I'll see you soon," he promised and then he was gone.

Beth stood on the porch, watching the taillights of the Nova disappear down the street. She wrapped her arms around herself and leaned against the porch rail, smiling softly.

Chapter Six

The kiss stayed on her mind the next day, and even two days later, as she climbed the rickety stairs into the attic of the Inn, a dreamy smile played at the corners of her lips. She had booked two additional reservations for the following week and one of her current guests wanted to extend their stay. She was going to have to open up another room and wanted to see what kind of furniture was lurking in the attic before she finished her shopping. She had only glanced briefly through the large open space when she bought the house, but she thought she remembered at least a dresser or two covered in dust among the boxes and trunks left over from days gone by.

She had certainly remembered the dust correctly. The space was covered with it and Beth sneezed as she walked across the spacious area. It was long and open, with a slanted ceiling. The floor had been reinforced with old wooden planks that were weathered from the years and the walls and ceiling were non-insulated beams.

While the attic was, for the most part, empty, there were numerous pieces of old furniture, mostly in a state of disrepair, and some boxes and old trunks scattered throughout the room. Beth examined a dresser and nightstand she found, running her hands over the warped wood. In contrast to the furniture that had been left in the house, these pieces were poorly constructed and had probably not been valuable even in their day. They seemed out of place with the opulent taste of the Latte family and she wondered if they might have belonged to some other family member, or one of the other owners.

Beth pulled open the drawers, but the pieces were empty. She didn't bother to look at the rest of the furniture. None of it would do for any of the main rooms in the house. She would have to scrap the whole lot later.

For curiosity's sake, she opened some of the old boxes and trunks. As she expected, they were filled with clothes long since disintegrated into mere scraps of material. She knelt and held a faded blue dress out for inspection. It was covered in holes and smelled musty and old.

"What a shame," she whispered in the silent room. These scraps were part of someone's history and no one had bothered to take care of them, leaving them in the cold dusty attic for years.

As she stood, her foot caught in a loose floorboard and she stumbled forward. Her ankle twisted painfully and she sat back down with a thump.

"Ouch. Ouch," she yelped, reaching for her leg. Her ankle throbbed, but after a moment, she was able to move it around.

She twisted around to find the offending floorboard. Sure enough, one piece, near the trunk she had opened, stuck up from the floor.

"Shame on you," she scolded, pushing at the rotten wood. "You could have really hurt me."

As she pushed at the wood, it broke away, revealing a small space beneath the floor.

"What on earth?" Beth leaned forward. Inside, in a small dark space located underneath the floor, was a stack of letters. They looked old and yellowed and were tied with a faded ribbon.

Beth reached down and removed the package. There appeared to be a dozen or so letters in all, but no envelopes, no addresses. Whatever those letters contained had never been sent--at least not through the postal service.

Very carefully, Beth untied the ribbon and unfolded the letter at the top of the stack. She was afraid the fragile paper would disintegrate at her touch. It felt chalky and stiff. The handwriting was faded and cracked, but the words were readable:

Oh, grief beyond all other grief. Why was I made? What do I have to live for? I do not exist without you.

Love,

Laurilee

Laurilee.

Beth's heartbeat sped to an alarming rate. After all the weeks of wondering, here it was, in writing--the name that haunted her.

Laurilee.

She was real.

One by one, straining to be careful with the delicate paper, Beth read through the letters as if reading Laurilee's life backwards.

...where are you? Why do you leave me here--alone--cold and frightened?...

...I watch you from the attic. I'm glad there is no one to see me suffer...

...I know that I have more than I deserve. You love me, don't you?...

...I know it is wrong, these feelings...

...You have been kind to me and I have learnt to love you...

Beth clutched the paper so tightly that she could feel her palms clench with the tension. It was as if in reading the letters, she felt Laurilee growing inside her. She felt the anguish poured forth from a wounded heart.

Who was this mystery man? Who was Laurilee? Why did she suffer so?

Realizing suddenly that she was cold, Beth curled herself into a ball, wrapping her arms around her knees. It wasn't just the words; it was as if Beth felt the emotions behind them. She literally felt as if someone she loved had been torn from her. She felt the loneliness and the heartache. Her stomach knotted painfully and she gasped for breath. She closed her eyes and rocked back and forth, scarcely aware that a low keening sound escaped from her mouth. Laurilee's departure had been traumatic. She had been alone and frightened--in a new place, away from everybody that she loved. A shadowy image filled her mind's eye. It was him--the man she loved.

Reaching out, she called to him...

She could almost see him...

Almost touch him...

Beth's eyes snapped open. She sat up in a flash, looking around in confusion. Where was she?

She blinked several times as if coming out of a fog. Looking around, she could see that she was still in the attic. She didn't know how long she'd been sitting there, curled up in a ball, but the sun was sinking outside, casting long shadows over the room.

Had she fallen asleep? Beth frowned and tried to remember. She felt tired, as if she was waking from a long nap, but she didn't think she had been asleep. It seemed like she had had a dream, but she couldn't remember any of the details.

Slowly, she stood, feeling lightheaded. After taking a moment to steady herself, Beth looked down and saw the group of letters still clutched in her hand. Her link to Laurilee. She wanted to read them again, searching for clues, but she felt exhausted. She would read them tonight before she went to bed. She started for the door and then stopped in her tracks.

The room grew cold and Beth knew, with an overwhelming sense of certainty that the letters were not meant to leave the attic. Turning, she walked, almost trance-like, back and placed the bundle back in the hidden space below the floor. She returned the broken board to its original position and left the room.

Outside the attic, Beth took a deep breath. She felt lighter now, more like her old self. She turned back to the attic door, frowning. It was silly to leave the letters in that dusty old attic. What had come over her? They didn't belong in the attic. She wanted to read them again.

Sharply, she turned and entered the attic. Inside the door, she hesitated, glancing around suspiciously for--oh, who knows--a gust of cold air maybe? But the room was still.

"Good," she said aloud and retrieved the letters, carrying them downstairs and leaving them on her nightstand to read later.

After supper, Beth was surprised by the doorbell. All of her clients had retired for the evening and she wasn't expecting anyone new.

"Oh, no, not another stranded pair of newlyweds." She grinned to herself as she answered the door.

It was Tom.

She hadn't seen him since the kiss and her pulse quickened at the sight of him. He must have just left the library because he was wearing his standard work uniform of khaki pants and a button down shirt. He looked very clean cut and handsome.

"Hi there," she said, surprised and pleased at his presence. She wondered if he would kiss her hello.

He didn't.

Instead he grinned at her and her heart melted.

"Hey." His cheeks were ruddy and red from the humidity. His hands were clasped behind his back and he rocked forward on the balls of his feet. His eyes glowed with the air of a mischievous schoolboy.

Beth became instantly wary and asked suspiciously, "What are you up to?"

She tried to peak around his shoulder to see what he was holding behind his back but Tom sidestepped her.

"Not so fast." He shook his head in mock warning. "First, you have to ask me about the hoe down."

"Hoe down?" Beth had no idea what he was talking about.

But, Tom nodded seriously. "Square dance. Whatever. At the Elks Lodge."

"The Elks Lodge."

"Uh huh," Tom nodded vigorously. "On Saturday."

"Saturday."

Tom laughed. "Are you going to repeat everything I say?"

"Maybe," Beth countered and then couldn't stop herself from asking, "All right... so what about this hoe down?"

"Square dance," Tom corrected and then repeated, "It's Saturday."

"At the Elks Lodge," Beth finished as a grin started on her face. "I remember."

Tom grinned back at her like a little boy. "Wanna go with me?"

Despite the perfectly grown up flutter in her stomach, Beth responded girlishly, "You mean like a date?"

Tom pursed his lips for a moment and then nodded eagerly. "Yeah, like that."

Beth crossed her arms over her chest and tilted her head. "I don't know. I have to think about it."

Tom rocked back on his heels and raised his eyebrows knowingly. "Well, I could always take Mrs. Graham. I bet she wouldn't have to think about it."

"I'll bet you're right." Beth burst into laughter. "I'd love to go," she announced, pleased and already looking forward to spending time with Tom.

"Good," Tom said, his pleasure showing in his bright eyes. "I'll break the news to Mrs. Graham."

They laughed again and Beth stepped aside, saying in a rush, "I'm sorry--making you stand on the porch. Do you want to come inside?"

As Tom followed her into the parlor, he said nonchalantly, "Oh, by the way, look what I found."

Beth turned to see Tom holding out his hands, which contained a stack of weathered and yellowed newspapers.

Seeing their tenuous state, she made a face and stepped away from them. "Recycling, are you?"

"No, look," he pushed the stack toward her and she was forced to accept the bundle.

Turning around the papers, she noted the heading for the Garden Ridge Gazette. The date was 1950.

"Wow. Where did you find these?" Beth skimmed through the paper idly. Her mind continued to wander to thoughts of kissing.

Tom replied seriously, "They were in the Archives Room."

Beth looked up and raised an eyebrow doubtfully. "The Archive Room?"

"At the library." Tom shrugged modestly. "We don't throw much away around there."

"Sounds like a fire hazard to me," Beth retorted dryly.

Tom snatched at the paper. "If you don't want them…"

Holding the papers out of his reach, she asked suspiciously, "Why would I be interested in these? I wasn't even born in 1950."

Feigning innocence, he shrugged, "Oh, I don't know. Maybe because a certain very prominent family was around in 1950. A family that you might share something like, oh, say, a house, in common with."

"The Latte's?" Beth snapped her attention back to the paper. Finally a topic more distracting than kissing Tom.

As she skimmed the articles, Tom watched her. Truth was he had been looking for an excuse to see her again. He figured if he found some history, some piece of trivia, on the house, she'd have to let him in. As a result, he'd spent all day tracking through newspaper copies, searching for pertinent information.

Looking at her sitting next to him, her loose hair spilling across her face in soft amber curls as she flipped through the newspapers, he knew it had not been a waste of time. Her skin, light and delicate, glowed in the dim light of the room. He knew from holding her at the movie, how well that body fit next to his; how each of her curves molded into his. He wanted to take her in his arms again and feel her softness…

"This is incredible."

Her soft voice stirred him from his reverie and Tom leaned forward. She was pointing to a small picture in the social column. "Matthew Latte."

She scrambled up and reached for the history book Tom had leant her and opened to the picture of James Latte.

"Look," she compared the pictures. There was clearly a family resemblance in the sharp, pointed features of the man. "That must be his grandson."

A short article followed, mentioning a charity event. She skimmed it with interest, remarking, "I imagine Jonathon bore the resemblance as well. The book said that Jonathon ran the plantation and kept it profitable throughout his lifetime."

"I read in one of those articles that Jonathon's mother ran the household until she died," Tom offered.

"Really?" Beth cocked her head to one side as if she were thinking back. She remarked conversationally, "I didn't think they got along."

Tom frowned. "Why would you think that? I didn't read anything about any family feuds."

"It wasn't a feud," she corrected, turning back to the stack of newspapers. "He just didn't feel comfortable around her. Especially after his father died."

Tom's frown remained. "I did read that James Latte died young, but I don't recall any details."

"It was a broken heart," Beth said evenly, browsing through the papers.

"What?" Tom sounded more confused than ever. "Are you making this up?"

Beth looked up from the paper as if she'd just heard him for the first time. "What?"

"I asked if you were making this up," Tom repeated.

"No." Beth tapped the book. "It says right here Jonathon ran the plantation, keeping it profitable throughout his lifetime. I think it was Matthew that finally sold the house."

"I was talking about..." Tom let the sentence trail off. Of course she was making it up. "Never mind."

Beth gave him a strange look and went back to the article she was reading. "I wish I knew more about them."

"The Latte's?" Tom asked.

Beth nodded. "What do you think happened to them?"

Tom shrugged. "I don't know. I guess the same thing that happens to every family. The parents died, the children grew up and the grandkids moved away."

Beth turned to him. "Maybe it was something more dramatic. What if the family was devastated by some tragic event that haunted them and tore them apart? And then the house carried the secret for years, harboring it until it grew so big that it couldn't be contained inside the house any longer?"

Tom made a disbelieving face. "Don't you think there'd be some sort of documentation if something tragic had happened?"

Beth shrugged. "What if it happened a really long time ago? You know, the power company just wanted the land to put a right of way through the property. They never occupied the house. That's why it is in such good shape. No one's lived in it since Matthew Latte moved out."

She looked at him expectantly. He didn't know what to say. His mind whirled with the information she'd tossed out, spinning her idea into a story as only a true novelist could. It did have all the makings of a true ghost tale. Tom had to physically fight the urge to run home and put his thoughts on paper--a feeling he hadn't had in a long time.

But, looking at Beth, so innocent and vulnerable, he knew that he would not share his true thoughts. Instead, he nodded, giving every indication that he did not take her tale seriously. "I didn't realize that you had such a dramatic flair."

"It could have happened," Beth mused and then asked, "I know that you don't believe in ghosts per se; but, do you think that a person's energy can remain somewhere after they leave?"

Tom's instincts perked up. "I don't know. Do you?"

"Maybe." Beth sat for a moment and then looked directly into Tom's eyes and asked very, very quietly. "You don't think this house is haunted, do you?"

"Haunted?" Tom repeated, stalling for time. He couldn't believe the nature of this conversation. It was a verbal outline of a novel. He wanted desperately to pursue it, but he didn't want to upset Beth, either. Instead of answering, he looked at her intently, and asked, "Do you?"

Beth thought for a moment and then looked around, wrapping her arms around her chest. "No. It's just that, I guess, as we've said all along, the house isn't very different from when the Lattes lived here."

Tom could picture the large house, with its incredible history, as the centerpiece of something big. Already bits and pieces of a story were forming together in his mind. He didn't want to scare her, but he couldn't help but prompt, "Is this about the lady from the welcome party? The one who heard noises in the garden?"

Beth turned a little too sharply and said a little too quickly. "That was the wind."

"Okay." Tom backed off, but saw the doubt in her eyes. "Has anything else unusual happened?"

Beth thought about the shadow in the window. The dream. The whispers. And the letters. Especially about the letters. Then she shook her head in frustration and returned to the sofa. "No," she denied quickly. "It's the old house. It creaks."

She ran her hands over the book and newspapers on the coffee table. The Lattes had become real to her somehow. And Laurilee.

"A lot of people believe in them, you know." Tom dug a little further. "They claim to see them, or hear them, or feel them--like a presence in the room or the feeling that someone was watching from an empty window."

"Stop." Beth practically shouted the word. He was hitting too close to home. At his shocked expression, she added. "I don't have ghosts."

"I wasn't suggesting that you have ghosts." Tom suddenly felt a little defensive. "I was just saying that people do believe in them."

Beth said with a touch of sarcasm. "I know… I saw the room in the library. There were books all over the place."

"There are a lot of people who are very interested in the subject." He didn't mention that he was one of those people.

Now, Beth rolled her eyes. "I don't even know what a ghost is."

Although she sounded like she was kidding, there was seriousness in her expression that Tom picked up immediately. She might not be ready to share the details with him, but Tom sensed some underlying reason for that comment. Luckily for her, he was the right person to ask. Keeping his explanation to the bare minimum, he said, "Technically, I would say a ghost is a material being without a physical occupant."

"What does that mean?" She hadn't meant to prolong the conversation, but she suddenly realized that Tom had information that she wanted. She wanted to know more about the subject and if Tom were willing to share that information, maybe it would give her some answers. Tom thought for a moment and then tried again. "In other words, a person from which all physical components, like flesh and bones, have been removed, yet all other characteristics by which that person is perceived, including their personality or soul have survived. What remains would be the ghost or apparition."

It was a technical explanation and Beth didn't put too much thought into it. With a fearful heart, she asked the real question burning in her mind.

"What do they want?"

Tom wanted to reach out and touch her, comfort her somehow, but he sensed her distance and, instead, answered her question to the best of his ability. "According to ghost stories of the 17th century, most phantoms returned to earth to give a warning, or to advise or haunt mortals, to confess their guilt or sins, to provide for their heirs by telling where treasures were hidden or to seek revenge, right a wrong or obtain justice."

"She sinned."

Beth's voice was the smallest of whispers and Tom leaned forward, unsure that he had heard her correctly. "I'm sorry. Who sinned?"

Beth turned back to him innocently. "What?"

Tom watched her intently. "It sounded like you said she sinned."

Beth shook her head, frowning, "I don't think so." She leaned forward and closed the book on the coffee table. It made a loud snap in the quiet room. "Thanks for the information." She smiled at him lightly. "For someone who doesn't believe in ghosts, you sure know a lot about the subject."

Tom felt a stab of guilt pierce his soul. He should tell her the truth. He knew the information because he was a writer. He wrote ghost stories.

Or at least he used to. If she were to ask to read his latest work, he'd have little to show but a dusty keyboard. His new manuscript, what little of it survived the delete key, was garbage. His reputation was based solely on his unique ability to scare the public with the written word. His stories were bizarre and scary. His audiences loved them. They expected nothing less than to be scared witless with each new story. Each tale had to be bigger and more horrifying than the last.

For the last two years, he'd churned out the same old lines. The same tired plots. He didn't have anything new. Anything different. He had lost his edge. It was clear from his latest efforts and he'd felt it in his core.

Until now. Talking about ghosts like that stirred up something in his soul. Plots and paragraphs swirled around his mind, overtaking his common sense. He had to get home and put this down on paper. He knew the feeling and he couldn't let it go.

Standing up, he smiled a distracted smile in Beth's direction. "I'm a book person. I know a lot about every subject." She didn't seem to hear or care about his answer as she stared into the distance. He took a step towards the door. "I'll see you tomorrow, okay?"

Beth barely nodded, her mind clearly elsewhere. Any other day, Tom would have stopped everything to make sure she was okay, but the writer, Sam Shelling, took over, leading him home.

After Tom left, Beth returned to her bedroom. In the aftermath of his departure, the fact that Tom had not attempted any sort of intimate contact, in word or gesture, created a very strong feeling of despondence. Beth was depressed and craved solace. Somebody who could understand her longing and her confusion.

The bundle of letters on the nightstand drew her like a magnet. She withdrew one of the pages and studied the paper with a critical eye. The handwriting was cursive and flowing, indicative of the time. But, the sentences were short and stilted. The writing was most certainly feminine, but this was not a woman of many words.

Or an educated woman. Beth furrowed her eyebrows as she studied the faded ink. Although some of the words were distinct to the time period, and not altogether familiar to her, some words were clearly not spelled correctly. And the grammar seemed off.

Beth rubbed her temple, which had suddenly begun to pound from the intense scrutiny of the intricate letters. She snapped off the lamp and lay back, fully clothed, on the bed.

As her eyes closed, a vision danced before them. She could almost see a woman reaching for her, but she could not make out any details. It floated, shapeless, in the back of her mind.

In a flash, the vision was gone.

"Oh, Laurilee, who are you?" she cried into the darkness.

But, as expected, no one was there to answer.

Chapter Seven

The following week passed quickly at the Laurilee Inn. The day of the dance approached before Beth realized. She stood in the kitchen, looking out over the back yard with the sun barely risen. Lately, early morning was the only time she had to herself. She found herself increasingly busy as her guest list started to fill. The main house already had a waiting list for the busiest weeks of the summer and Beth figured she would probably have to start preliminary plans to begin conversion of the carriage house to accommodate her growing client base sooner than she had anticipated.

Luckily, she had good help. Rosie had been a godsend. Her cooking was superb and she loved the Inn almost as much as Beth.

Despite the increased occupancy at the Inn, or maybe because of it, Beth was relieved to find that there had been no middle-of-the-night complaints of phantom noises, even after she had to break down and start booking guests into the rooms overlooking the courtyard. The guests were happy and busy and in amour of her little house.

Even with the appearance of normalcy at the Inn, Beth could not bring herself to return Laurilee's letters to the attic. They remained in a bundle in the top drawer of her nightstand. On occasion, she took them out and read them, looking for clues; but, for the most part, Beth felt secure just knowing that they were close to her. Anyway, she was too busy running the Inn to give Laurilee much thought.

Too busy running the Inn and thinking about Tom Hartman that was. Somehow, she managed to spend most of her free time daydreaming about him.

And tonight she had a date with him. Not that she hadn't seen him plenty over the past week. He called her at least once a day and stopped by almost as often. He made her laugh and brought her little trinkets he thought she would enjoy. His manners were impeccable. He always held open the door and pulled out her chair. Please and Thank You were common phrases and he showed her plenty of affection. Touching her arm; holding her hand. They were perfectly comfortable together and got along famously.

But, tonight was different. It was a date. And that implied all kinds of possibilities.

Beth couldn't help but wonder what would happen if Tom threw caution to the wind and took her in his arms and kissed her passionately. She spent enough time fantasizing about it. However, as soon as she saw him in the flesh, she stiffened up and became the proper reserved Englishwoman.

It was a crying shame.

And Beth intended to do something about it.

Sometime.

Soon.

But, not before breakfast.

Tom munched on a piece of cold toast as he stared at his computer screen. He had been surprised to see the first glimmer of dawn peak through the window of his office. The last time he had checked, the late night talk show host had been in the middle of a monologue about current policies. Next to his computer, an impressive pile of typewritten paper had accumulated. It wasn't exactly an outline, but it was a collection of fairly cohesive thoughts and ideas that would eventually arrange themselves into a story. It was how he worked. Some writers spent months formulating a precise outline that would be followed specifically chapter by chapter in creating a book. Those same writers agonized over every word in the initial draft of the book, making sure that each word placement was exactly right. At the end, these writers had a book that required very little revision before publication.

Not Tom. He scattered a bunch of notes on paper and came up with a general idea in his head. He took that idea and then started with *Chapter One*. As he wrote, the characters took shape and sometimes morphed into completely different entities, taking on a life of their own. He allowed the characters to lead the way through the story, sometimes changing his ideas as he went along. He never knew, when he started a book, how it would end. That was the fun of it. He just let the characters lead the way. Of course, he then had to go back and adjust the initial chapters to make sure they flowed with the eventual end which took several revisions and drove his editors crazy; but that, also, was part of the fun.

For the first time in a long time, Tom felt good about his ideas. He had some really great notes and he knew he was close to typing the words Chapter One on his way to another best seller.

Tom swallowed the last of his toast and looked out the window. In the distance, he could see the peak of the Laurilee Inn at the end of the street. He felt a slight tug in his gut. All of his ideas centered around the concept of a southern plantation haunted by the past. It was unique and it was intriguing. He truly hoped Beth would understand how his ideas just came to him. Any similarities between his story and the Laurilee Inn were purely coincidental.

Because no one was saying that the Laurilee Inn was haunted.

This was purely fiction.

It had nothing to do with Beth. Or her captivating smile and sparkling eyes. Or those lips made to be kissed, if only she weren't so reserved. He could change that.

And he would.

Sometime.

Soon.

But, not before breakfast.

As night fell on the sleepy town, Beth stood uncertainly in front of the full length mirror in her bedroom. What exactly did one wear to a hoedown?

"I mean square dance," she giggled aloud.

She had put on a full linen skirt that swung past her knees with a fitted top and sandals. Probably cowboy boots would be more appropriate, but she didn't own any.

She fingered the red ribbon she found so often in her hair and then laid it on the counter. "Laurilee, you have to stay home this time."

There were no theatrics as Tom picked up Beth for the dance. He looked very clean-cut in starched blue jeans and a white button down shirt that complimented his dark hair and skin.

Beth felt shy, probably because of the errant ways of her thoughts over the past week, and was quiet on the short ride across town.

The Elks Lodge sat on a large tract of land on the other side of town. It was a large, rectangular building with wood floors and a large stage set up at one end. A band playing country music livened up the moods and several of the younger people danced in front of the stage.

Along the other side of the room, a huge buffet table had been set up. Beth smelled fried chicken and could see dishes of homemade sides filling up the table. She sighed, "I'm going to have to stay away from that table if I have any regard for my waistline."

"Oh, we'll dance off those calories in no time, "Tom laughed.

"Uh…" Beth started to remind him that she didn't know any country dance steps when a figure from the stage caught her eye. "Is that Mr. Carmello from the corner store?"

The older man, who ran the corner store, stood in the middle of the stage playing his fiddle. He looked very spry in a black cowboy hat and jeans, dancing a little jig as he played.

Tom nodded and commented, "Talented, isn't he?"

"He is," Beth agreed and then said thoughtfully, "I would not have pictured him as a fiddle player--he seems so reserved at the store. But, I guess everyone has a secret side."

Tom winced internally. But, he didn't want to spoil the evening, so he steered her in the direction of the buffet and off the topic of secrets.

"I can't eat another bite," Beth laughed thirty minutes later as she tossed her empty plate into the trash. "Some of these ladies would give Rosie a run for her money." She'd sampled collard greens, three different kinds of mashed potatoes, chicken, ham and about a half dozen versions of ambrosia salad. And there were still brownies, fudge and every flavor pie imaginable beckoning from the table.

As the evening progressed, the lodge filled up with exuberant locals of every age. The young couples danced, occasionally dashing out to the back deck where the beer kegs were located. They shared dance floor space with children and teenagers horsing around while their parents and grandparents sat around card tables, watching and gossiping.

Tom put his arm around Beth as they sat in a couple of folding chairs next to the dance floor. She seemed happy and relaxed. He grinned at her. "Bet you never went to a square dance growing up."

"That would be a pretty safe bet. The closest I got to dancing was the ballet."

But, she didn't feel sad when she said it. Maybe the little town was starting to have the desired effect on her. She was finally able to look back on her childhood with more of an appreciation. Now she smiled. "I used to love dressing up to go to the ballet. And afterwards, we'd go to a fancy restaurant and I'd feel so grown up-- even though I usually got confused over which utensil was proper for seafood."

"Don't have to worry about that here." Tom held up his plastic fork and Beth laughed.

Tom put down the fork and asked, "Was your family very rich?"

She looked sideways at him and he seemed genuinely curious so she answered honestly, "Yes, we were."

"What was it like, growing up that way?"

Beth sighed nostalgically. "When I was really young, I guess I didn't notice it. It didn't occur to me that spending all day with a nanny instead of my parents was unusual. And when I got a little older, I spent a great deal of time resenting that lifestyle. I didn't appreciate how lucky I was. Even after they were gone. I just wanted to escape all of it--the money and the lifestyle. I'm grateful for the opportunities, but I really want to succeed on my own."

Tom took her hand. "It must have been hard to lose your parents at such a young age."

"It was," she agreed and then tilted her head at him. "But, you know that as well as I."

Tom nodded. "My parents died when I was five. I was raised by my grandmother. Luckily for me, she was a loving, generous woman. Even though she died when I was a teenager, I had a very happy childhood."

"And yet you left," Beth commented.

"Yes, I did. I wanted to see the world."

"Did you?" Beth wanted to know.

"Some of it," Tom answered truthfully. After he finally sold a novel and his advances became more generous, he had taken the opportunity to travel. He owned an apartment in New York, where he used to travel regularly to see his agent and editors, but he hadn't been in a while, and a vacation home in Aspen. In a storage facility in New York, he kept a Ferrari and a Range Rover. But, all of that seemed very distant to him now.

As if reading his mind, Beth added, "And then you came back."

"Yes, I did," he replied again. He had lived a lavish lifestyle for a while, but the stones kept pulling him back to Georgia. He owned a ranch in west Georgia, but he hadn't been there in over a year. He sighed, "I guess the world wasn't all that I thought it would be."

It was the most truthful statement he had made in a long time.

She leaned in to him and put her head on his shoulder. "You know, I think there is something about this town that makes everything seem easier. I haven't felt this peaceful in a long time. I don't need any material things. I have my bed and breakfast and I love this small town life."

As she said the words, she wondered if it was the town or if it was Tom. He made her feel safe and protected. Maybe, he was what she had been missing.

The band started up a slow waltz and Beth took Tom's hand. "I think it's about time you taught me some of those country dance steps."

To him, her voice was low and seductive. She didn't have to tell him twice. He had been daydreaming about holding her in his arms all night.

They moved to the dance floor and he took her, wrapped his arms around her, and folded her into him. They swayed together in time to the music and the rest of the crowd faded away. Her body molded perfectly into his, each of her curves finding a matching contour in Tom.

She laid her head on his shoulder and he smelled the sweet essence of her perfume. It was soft and floral like her and his heart rate picked up just at the scent of it. She rested one arm around his neck while he held the other in his hand. The softness of her body pressed so close to him sent his own body burning with desire and he could see by the tiny pulse in her neck that she felt the same way.

The spark they had both felt over the months ignited as they danced, heating to a deep, glowing ember. Beth raised her head and looked into Tom's eyes, smoky with desire. She tilted her head ever so slightly on one side, allowing Tom the opportunity to kiss her if he wanted.

Oblivious to anything around him, Tom pressed his lips to hers, savoring their softness. Beth moved her hand from his neck to his cheek, placing it gently on his jaw line. Her skin was warm and his face flamed at her touch. He breathed deeply and kissed her again, careful to remember that they were still in public.

She accepted his kiss like a starving woman. Tom's kiss was so much more than she could have ever dreamed. It was as if he poured his soul into the simple act. Her entire body felt the effect of his lips on her mouth. It was all consuming and Beth could only imagine what his lovemaking would be like. As those thoughts filled her mind, Beth shifted her body slightly against his. The move was subtle enough that no one watching would notice, but she immediately felt his body respond.

"You are driving me crazy," he whispered against her so that no one else could hear.

Beth lifted her head and looked at him. Their faces were very close and she could feel the heat radiating between them. They stood that way, wrapped up in each other, physically and emotionally, until the last strum of the guitar faded from the song.

Aware of the eyes on them, Beth took a step back and said with only a slight tremor in her voice. "I think Mrs. Graham is staring daggers though my back."

"I think that's me undressing you with my eyes." Tom's intimate smile went straight to her heart.

"Oh," Beth raised a hand to her mouth as her cheeks flushed. "Well, I guess that's okay, then."

As the band started the next song, the couple left the dance floor. But, suddenly, the lively gathering had lost some of its appeal. Beth and Tom were lost in each other. They said hasty good-byes amongst knowing glances and drove quickly back to Beth's.

Her guests had retired to their rooms, and Beth and Tom sat quietly in the parlor, holding hands. The newfound heat overlying their natural chemistry was an explosive mix. They made out on the sofa like school children. They explored the new depth of their feelings, alternately heating up with passion and giggling and whispering in the darkness.

Beth couldn't remember ever being happier.

When, hours later, they kissed good-bye at the door, Beth knew that something within her had changed forever.

As the sun rose over the sleepy town, Tom sat in front of the computer reading the last paragraph on the screen. He hadn't slept after leaving Beth. His body sizzled with emotion and desire. It had taken all of his restraint to leave Beth, but he respected her too much to allow anything further to happen when he was hiding so much from her. Even as he typed, he felt incredibly guilty at his deception. She needed to know who he was and what he did for a living. But, would she see him in the same way? He didn't want to take a chance on losing her--her friendship and where that friendship was heading. If he could just get one more novel working--something big-- something he could be proud of.

Then the truth could come out.

Chapter Eight

The next morning, Beth inhaled the aroma of freshly baked biscuits, sizzling ham and bacon and brewing coffee. In a matter of minutes, the kitchen would be full of appreciative breakfast eaters.

As soon as the thought cleared her mind, Beth heard footsteps on the back stairway. She looked up from the newspaper she was reading and greeted her guest with a smile. "Morning, Helen. You're up early."

Helen poured a cup of coffee and nodded. "I wanted to get an early start. I'm going shopping for antiques today. Bill wants to stay in and watch the game."

Unlike the newlywed couples that often frequented the Inn, Helen and Bill had been married for over twenty years. Childless, they spent several months a year traveling whenever the mood hit and didn't feel the need to spend every moment together. Helen had already been on several excursions while her husband relaxed in the cozy parlor watching the big screen TV and both seemed perfectly agreeable to the setup.

Now Beth smiled. "Make sure to hit Avenue B. There are some great little stores."

"I will." Helen grinned and finished off her coffee before rising from the table.

"Will you stay for breakfast? We have ham and egg omelets," Beth offered as she returned her attention to the article she was reading, but Helen shook her head.

"I'll pick up something on the way. By the way," Helen paused she was about to leave the kitchen. "I'd love to meet your kids sometime."

Distracted by the newspaper, Beth answered absently, "Oh, I don't have any children."

Helen paused and tilted her head to one side, saying absently, "That's funny. I can hear them playing in the courtyard almost every afternoon."

Beth's heart stopped. The familiar chill crawled along her spine as the words sank in. Taking a deep breath she began her usual speech, trying to keep her voice light. "You know, the wind in the courtyard makes the funniest sounds. People are always saying…"

"No." Helen stopped her mid-speech, with the firm, but gentle, word. "I'm sure of what I heard."

Before Beth could continue her protest, Helen waved a hand in the air. "But, I have very sensitive physic abilities. Maybe I'm hearing children from the past."

The words struck Beth dumb. Children from the past?

"What do you mean?" She asked, afraid to hear the answer.

Helen shrugged easily, "I often see or hear things that other people can't. I'm used to it by now, although, every once in a while, I'll get a sense of something really bad and it's not very fun."

Beth's heart sank. Was this really bad? She couldn't afford to start losing customers again. With a downtrodden voice, she asked, "Are you going to leave?" The Banks were scheduled for three more days and she didn't want any more guests abandoning the Inn.

But, again, Helen shook her head easily. "Your Inn is lovely. And the children are friendly. I see no reason to leave."

"The children are friendly?" Beth couldn't stop herself from asking.

Helen regarded her for a moment, trying to read her expression. Then, she smiled and nodded. "Oh, yes. I hear them laughing and playing in the courtyard. They seem to be having a wonderful time."

Beth frowned and nodded, lost in thought over the image Helen created. Why didn't she hear the children? And were they connected to Laurilee? A thousand questions ran though her mind. Maybe this woman, a psychic, could provide some of the answers. She opened her mouth to ask another question and then snapped it shut, shaking her head.

Helen reached out a hand to touch Beth's arm. "Is there something else?"

"No." This time Beth shook her head immediately. No sense scaring the guests, even psychic ones. She smiled graciously at the woman. "Enjoy the rest of your day."

"I will." Helen smiled back and headed out the back door.

Beth took a deep breath, but felt only momentary relief. Just because the Banks' were going to stay didn't mean others would. She had to find out exactly what was going on at her Inn.

The only clue she had so far were the letters, but they didn't mention children. Only loneliness and despair.

Beth went upstairs. She wanted to read the letters again; to search for the missing piece. The piece that would tell her where Laurilee fit in. And the children.

As she reached into the nightstand, Beth felt her hands shake. It was only paper, but her heart thumped as if she were reaching into a den of live snakes. She touched the faded ribbon holding the bundle together and, as she had come to expect, a burst of freezing air rushed past her.

Laurilee had been waiting for her.

The air grew thick with her presence. Maybe it was her imagination, but Beth could swear that the faint scent of perfume filled the air. It grew stronger, a deep lavender scent that seemed thick and dated, not like the light floral scent that Beth sprayed on herself each morning.

Keeping her hand on the letters, somehow certain that they were the link to Laurilee, Beth asked aloud, her voice shaking, "Laurilee?"

There was no anger in her voice, like before, no threat, just the pregnant pause of expectation. Silence filled the air, but Beth knew by the thickness around that Laurilee was still there.

She waited.

"The children…"

The whisper was a cold breeze floating across the room, but the words were unmistakable.

"The children…"

"What about the children?" Beth stood frozen in the room, one hand gripping the letters so tightly that her knuckles where white, the other hand at her throat, feeling the sharp intake of each shaky breath. Her heart pounded like a drum in the silence of the room. Beads of sweat trickled down her forehead and along her stomach.

"My children…"

As suddenly as it came, the presence was gone. The air grew light and the smell of perfume faded into the light floral scent of her potpourri.

Beth collapsed onto the bed, letting the bundle of letters fall to the ground. She felt spent, as if she'd run a marathon or climbed a mountain. If she tried to stand, she was certain that her legs would crumple beneath her. Her skin felt hot and feverish and her breath came in short, painful rasps. Her arms and back ached as if she had lifted a heavy weight. Or held an awkward position for a long time.

Beth frowned. She felt stiff and sore all over. She rolled her neck, which creaked with movement. As she turned her head from side to side, she caught a glance at the clock on her dresser.

It read 10:30 AM. Immediately, she sat up, ignoring the stiffness in her muscles.

Impossible. She'd left the kitchen no later than 8:30 AM. Just after Helen left.

She picked up the clock and examined it closely. It seemed to be running fine. Then she glanced at the watch on her wrist. Also, 10:30 AM.

How could that be? She had just come into the room a minute ago.

Hadn't she?

Beth ran down the stairs, wincing as her leg muscles protested the rapid movements. In the kitchen, dishes were stacked in the sink and the newspaper sat folded on the table. Her guests had already had breakfast and gone about their daily activities. Upstairs, Rosie's footsteps could be heard as she went about her morning duties.

It was really two hours later.

Beth sank into one of the kitchen chairs. Something had happened in that bedroom today. Something she was no longer prepared to handle on her own.

With shaking hands, she reached for the phone.

Ten minutes later, Tom stood in her doorway, concern written all over his handsome face.

"Your face is flushed." He held a hand to her forehead. "Are you running a fever?"

Beth shook her head impatiently. "I'm not sick." At least not physically, she added silently.

Tom took her arm to lead her into the parlor, but Beth shook her head. The muffled sound of the TV could be heard. She didn't want her guests to overhear.

She led him upstairs to her bedroom, closing the door behind them. As if she were in tune with Laurilee now, she knew that the ghost would not make an appearance with Tom in the room.

Taking a deep breath, she sat on the bed facing Tom. She didn't know where to begin, or how much to divulge, but she had to tell someone. She was starting to get, maybe not scared, but worried.

Tom's eyes were warm and kind, full of caring and concern as he watched her.

"Okay," she clasped her hands together, "this morning, another guest, Helen Banks, came to me and told me she could hear children playing in the courtyard."

"Beth," Tom started, but Beth held up a hand.

"I know. I started to give her the usual explanation, but then she told me she had psychic abilities and that maybe she was hearing children from the past." She finished her sentence and looked at him hopefully.

"Beth, there are no such things as ghosts." His voice was gentle, but firm.

Beth raised her eyes to his, hers large and blue and looking for reassurance in his calm gray ones. "Are you sure?"

A spark caught in Tom's eye. His interest peaked. He took her hand. It was ice cold. He kept his voice soft. "Are you?"

A long second passed and then, slowly, Beth shook her head. She got up from the bed and went to the nightstand. She felt a terrible pull against her. It wasn't so much that she felt a presence in the room; but, she knew, without a doubt, that Laurilee didn't want her to share the letters.

"I have to," she whispered into the empty air and opened the drawer.

In deference to Laurilee, Beth removed only one letter and handed it to Tom. It was a short note.

Taking the folded paper from her, Tom read it.

My darling,
I am glad you took time to visit me today.
My soul fills with joy to see you.
I watch you from my room – I know you won't see me.
I am careful.
I pray to the Lord to send you to me again soon.
Laurilee.

Finished, he handed it back wordlessly.

Beth carefully inserted the letter into its rightful place in the stack and returned the bundle to her nightstand. Then she returned to her spot on the bed next to Tom and said, unable to keep the anguish from her voice, "I have to find her."

"Beth," Tom frowned as he looked at her, "that letter looked pretty old. I don't think she's still alive."

"She's not," Beth confirmed immediately, not exactly knowing where her words came from, "but, she's not dead, either. She can't rest. She has to find out the truth." Her sentences shot out in rapid succession as she continued, unable to control the flow of her words. "She has to find her children."

Beth's eyes glazed over and she stood from the bed, pacing the floor. She wrung her hands together in agitation.

Tom touched her shoulder

"Beth…"

Beth looked right at him. He knew she didn't see him. Her face twisted with anguish. And her mouth worked soundlessly. As he watched, Tom felt her features alter, as if she were taking on someone else's appearance. Someone helpless and scared. And angry.

"Beth," he shouted, his voice sharp and stern. He shook her. Hard. "Beth, stop."

The sharp command halted Beth in her tracks. Her knees went weak and she slumped to the floor. A second later, she opened her eyes and looked at him in confusion. "Why am I on the floor?"

Tom felt intimidated by the past several minutes. He didn't want to scare Beth. She genuinely seemed not to know what had happened to her. He shook his head lightly and said, "Happens all the time. Women falling at my feet like that."

She smiled thinly at his joke. "Was I out long?"

Although she looked confused, she didn't seem very surprised at the notion that she might have blacked out. Tom suspected that this had happened before.

He didn't like that idea.

He shook his head. "Barely a second." He didn't mention her glazed eyes and agitated pacing. He knew she didn't remember.

Then he met her gaze frankly. "Has this happened before?"

Beth was quiet for a long time. Then she nodded slowly. "I think so."

"Do you remember anything?"

This time Beth shook her head immediately. "No." Then she lowered her voice. "It's her, though. Laurilee."

"Who is Laurilee?" Tom asked, still confused on that issue.

"I don't know," she flung back at him in irritation. "But, she is here in my house and she wants something from me." She exhaled a giant breath and sat down hard on the bed.

Tom frowned and sat back down on the bed next to her. He purposely kept his voice quiet and non-threatening. "Are you sure about this?"

She seemed upset by this question and the doubts she obviously read in his eyes. Showing the stubborn fire that belonged to the true Beth Willis, she flung back at him probably with more intensity than she really felt, "Yes, I'm sure." She took a deep, passionate breath. "I'm not asking you to believe me, Tom. But, I know what I saw."

Instinctively, Tom believed that she wasn't lying.

As much as he knew about the subject, he'd always suspected that most of the stories he heard were exaggerated at least. Embellished to impress him. Or make a better story. But, Beth didn't know who he was. She had nothing to gain by making up these events.

But, Tom knew he had everything to gain. The rough outline in his study had begun to take shape even before Beth handed him that letter. As she spoke, empty spaces were being filled in; vague impressions being completed. The story was taking on a life of its own and Tom was no longer sure he could stop it. Beth's facts mingled with his fiction, weaving a story line that swelled with the need for escape. Tom's fingers involuntarily clenched and fought the urge to run home to his computer.

Oblivious to his traitorous thoughts, Beth said simply, "I just need to find out who Laurilee is. I have to know what she wants." She gazed at him, imploring, "Can't you help me?"

Tom touched her arm lightly, his own mind whirling. "I don't know what you saw and I certainly can't explain it, but, I do believe you, Beth. And I'll do my best to help you."

"You will?"

Beth slumped against him, sighing in relief. "Oh, thank you, Tom."

He held her for a moment, selfishly enjoying the feel of her soft, warm skin against him. Her dark hair brushed against his cheek as he lay his head on top of hers. With one hand, he brushed it back away from her face, savoring the silky feel of the auburn curls. Her breathing was heavy and he could feel the rise and fall of her breasts as she pressed against him. They felt soft and pliant.

He closed his eyes and willed himself to remain calm.

He wanted to kiss her, to hold her in his arms like he possessed her, but he held himself back. She was feeling too vulnerable. No matter what he felt in his heart, he had to protect her. From herself. And from him.

Beth leaned against him and whispered, "I'm so lucky to know you."

"Yeah?" Tom replied, still caught up in the feeling of her next to him.

But, she sat up and looked at him, her eyes wide and innocent. "You listened to me. And you believed me. That means so much to me. In all my life, I've been invisible; but, with you, I'm alive. You are the most honest person I know and I feel grateful to have you in my life."

It was such a heartfelt statement and, from the expression on her face, not an easy one for Beth to make. Still, the jolt in Tom's gut was physical. His stomach clenched and he was forced to stand up and walk to the window. Further contact would only cause him to break down and tell Beth everything.

Ignoring the sudden rapid beating of his heart, Tom looked out the window and counted to ten in his head in an attempt to regain his composure.

What could he say to her? That he loved her? He did, but that hardly mattered. Announcing the sudden revelation wasn't going to help Beth's situation. Or his own, for that matter. He had his own demons to contend with.

Was he going to tell her the truth about himself? That he was a famous writer caught up in exactly the lifestyle she was running from? She would hate him.

He needed the novel. Once he was back on top--confident in his abilities--he could explain everything to her.

And she would understand.

And everything would be okay.

Chapter Nine

Beth stared at Tom's back for what seemed like an eternity. He stood perfectly still, but she could see his fingers drumming on the windowsill, a sure sign that he was uncomfortable.

She cleared her throat and said, "I'm sorry... I shouldn't have said that."

Her voice trembled and she felt close to tears. It had been hard to open up, even just a little, and she felt hurt and rejected.

But, Tom turned from the window and went to kneel in front of her, taking both of her hands in his. "Don't you dare be sorry. I'm honored that you feel comfortable confiding in me. And I would never do anything to hurt you." His voice sounded strong and compelling as he tilted her chin upward, his eyes staring into hers. "Beth, I'm here to help you. I want to help you."

Beth listened to his words, but still noted the reserve in his eyes. He was holding something back. She could feel it. And she was learning very quickly to trust her instincts.

She nodded her head and pulled her hands from his grasp. She needed to take things back to a comfortable level. Maybe talk about something safe instead of her feelings for Tom. It was clearly not a subject he was ready to discuss. "So, about Laurilee... do you think I can find out who she was?"

Tom heard the disappointment in her voice. She was trying to be brave, but he had obviously hurt her feelings. He didn't know what to say to make her feel better. Not without opening up a whole can of worms. She was right, it was better to stay on a safer topic.

Plus, Sam Shelling was dying to know more about Laurilee.

Taking a deep breath, he said to Beth, "You said you found those letters in the attic?"

She nodded. "About two months ago." She paused and then added, "I haven't been back up since."

"Well," Tom said, his mind working with a writer's fury, thinking of gathering more information as research, "I think we should go back up to the attic and see if there were any more letters."

Again, a pause, but eventually Beth stood up and brushed off the front of her blue jeans. "I suppose you're right." She clapped her hands together once and attempted a too bright smile. "I guess no time like the present."

The attic was exactly as she left it. The dusty furniture. The warped floor boards. Beth led Tom to the crawl space in the floor where she had found the stack of letters, explaining, "I was walking back from the dresser and I tripped over the broken wood."

Tom knelt and reached underneath the floorboard. The tiny space was small and square.

"Nothing else there," he announced, standing up.

Beth nodded. She had expected as much.

"Did you go through the furniture?"

Beth shrugged. "Some of it. I was planning to trash the whole lot at some point."

"I think we should start there." Tom moved to the nearest dresser.

Together, they rifled through every piece of furniture and every box in the attic. While initially, it hadn't seemed like much, the better part of an hour passed quickly as drawers were opened and boxes overturned. Layers of dust rose in protest as objects were moved and shuffled.

Beth sneezed and rubbed her eyes. She sat surrounded by piles of old clothes pulled from a box. The smell in the air was thick with dust. She lifted an old apron, yellowed and moth-eaten, holding the garment between two fingers. "These things are awful. I didn't realize there was so much junk."

"It's amazing what kind of things can accumulate," Tom agreed. The dresser he was poking around in a far corner of the room muffled his voice.

"Hey, I found something."

Beth jumped up and ran over. Tom stepped out from behind the dresser holding a large dark object. Beth took a step closer. It looked like a book of some sort. "What is it?"

"It's an album." Tom opened the worn cover of the book. Inside, fastened to worn yellow pages with small pieces of tape turned brown by the years, were photographs. It wasn't a complete album. Only a half dozen or so pages filled the album. Not every page had a photo on it at all. It was easy to see where photos had been removed and not replaced.

It didn't matter. Beth felt her heart pound in anticipation. It was a start.

The pictures were all black and white, naturally. There were less than a dozen in all, most of them pictures of the house or the land around it.

Beth smiled softly. "So, this is the Laurilee Inn when she was young."

The house looked the same, even in the grainy black and white photos. The elaborate landscaping, of course, did not exist; the front yard was large and barren. The massive oak trees surrounding the property now were merely young saplings in the pictures. The house looked stark without its familiar surroundings, but basically the same.

"There's James," Beth exclaimed as they turned the page. He was standing in front of the house with another man and a boy.

James wore light riding breeches, a dark vest and long topcoat. His expression was stern and serious. The boy was dressed in similar fashion, but he stood with one hand on his hip and one ankle crossed over the other, as if he were about to skip off to play. He wore a jaunty smile and seemed to be up to some sort of mischief. He resembled James, standing to his left; both had dark hair and eyes; but, where the older man had pale, light skin, the boy's skin glowed with an olive hue.

Beth felt a tremor course through her as she looked at the picture of the boy. Something tugged at her heart and she smiled softly, feeling the inexplicable prick of tears at the back of her eyelids.

Tom turned the page.

The next picture showed James and Malthilde. James wore dark pants, a dark coat and a top hat. In his hand was a cane. Mattie sported an elaborate gown, fitted along her narrow waist and flaring out atop wide petticoats. Despite the sophisticated gown, it was easy to see the strong masculine features of James' wife. Her dark hair was pulled back into a severe bun, emphasizing her strong jaw and wide-set eyes. She was small in stature, yet wide along the shoulders and hips. Only her waist was narrow, pulled in by the stringent corset worn by the ladies of the time. Like her husband, her skin was light and pale, made even more so by the heavy white powder and dark lipstick apparent even in the photograph. Also, like her husband, she did not smile into the camera. The couple stood side by side, not touching, staring directly ahead with no hint of expression on either face.

Beth pulled away from the picture. Her heart raced inexplicably and she felt tears prick her eyes again.

"Not too attractive, huh?" Tom commented.

It was more than physical to Beth. The woman had raised a sense of fear in Beth, or intimidation, at least.

"She was mean," Beth blurted, not truly understanding her words, but feeling them with every ounce of her being.

"You think?" Tom, not hearing the emotion in her voice, studied the picture a little closer. "I guess she does have kind of a stern look, doesn't she?" Then he added casually, "But, I don't think you were supposed to smile at the camera back then."

Misreading her look of doubt, he added, "Remember, picture-taking was a luxury in those days. Most people thought the camera was just a fluke that would disappear within a couple of years."

"It wasn't the camera," Beth stated flatly and then turned the page.

Tom gave her a raised eyebrow look, but refrained from commenting.

A family photo followed. James and Mattie stood side by side, again straight-faced and serious. In front of them stood two children. The same boy from the previous picture and a girl, younger, but not by much, with long dark hair and olive skin. Unlike their parents, the kids stood, elbows touching, ankles crossed. While neither child smiled, per se, their expressions were lively and they seemed to be highly amused at the idea of being in the picture.

The picture had been taken behind the house. The old carriage house was in plain view, along with another structure that no longer existed.

"That must have been the kitchen," Tom remarked when Beth pointed out the structure. "The servants cooked the meals outside and then carried the food into the dining room to be served to the family."

Beth nodded. She remembered reading something to that effect in one of her old history books.

Then something else caught her eye. She leaned forward, staring hard. "Tom, look."

In the background of the picture, partially hidden by the family, stood a woman carrying a water pitcher. She was a servant, clothed in a plain cotton dress that hung loosely on a thin frame. She was tall by the standards of the day. Even though she stood behind the family, she towered over Mattie and seemed to be almost the same height as James. Her hair was long and straight and hung loosely down her back although it occurred to Beth that the servants would have been required to confine their hair in a bun. Despite the poor quality of the photograph, it was clear that this woman was strikingly beautiful.

She seemed to be walking from the kitchen towards the main house. Obviously unaware of the purpose of the photographer, she stared straight at the family before her. Her eyes, huge even in the grainy picture, looked large and sad as she watched the family posing.

Beth, tears streaming down her face, reached out to touch the picture.

"What is it?" Tom cried, alarmed by the sudden tears.

He started to close the book, but Beth placed her hand on top of his, keeping the book open.

"It's her," Beth murmured. She took the picture from the album, mindless of the disintegration of the page that held it. Her touch was almost a caress as she gently held the photo up. "It's Laurilee."

She was aware of the chill in the room, but felt no cold. It was right for Laurilee to be here. This was her story.

Tom took the picture from her and examined it. "How can you tell?"

"She's here. In the room." Beth's voice dropped to a whisper. The smell of lavender invaded her nostrils.

She stood up and began walking across the room. Tom scrambled to his feet, hurrying after her. "Where, Beth? I don't see anything." He looked around the room wildly. "There's nothing here."

Ignoring him, Beth stopped in front of an old trunk. Instead of picking through delicately and with distaste as she had done before, Beth rifled through a number of items from the trunk until she came across a faded blue shawl. Beth wrapped the large crochet needlepoint shawl around her shoulders, where it hung in tatters almost to the ground.

She walked to the window and stared out across the yard.

"Beth," Tom walked over to her. He immediately noticed the vague, unfocused glaze in her eyes. She was crying silently as she looked out the window.

She pressed her fingertips against the glass pane, her eyes scanning the yard below. Her breaths came in slow deep gasps and she seemed to be looking for something. When she found it, her posture straightened and she flattened her palm against the window. She seemed to lean forward, silently willing whatever she saw to notice her.

Tom stood beside her. There was nothing in the yard. He knew that already, but he looked anyway. When Beth started to mumble incoherently, he pulled her from the window.

He turned her around with ease, but she turned her head back to the window, straining for a glimpse of whatever held her attention.

"No." He turned her back to him and shook her hard. "Look at me, Beth."

It was a command and he practically shouted her name. He was afraid that if she fell too far into whatever trance held her, he might not be able to get her back.

Acting purely on instinct, he pulled her to him, crushing her lips against his. She stiffened momentarily and then moved her lips against his.

He pulled back for an instant, looking at her face. "Beth?"

Was he kissing Beth or someone else?

He knew he should stop. He had to be strong. But, her soft lips drove him into a state of frenzy. He looked at her, searching.

Beth saw the question in his eye. She knew she had gone somewhere just now, somewhere with Laurilee, but she was back and Tom was kissing her. She wasn't about to let him go.

To show him she was completely in the present, she stepped back and removed her hands from the tattered shawl. It fell to the floor, surrounding her feet in a pile of blue.

Tom understood the gesture. He wrapped his fingers in her dark hair and pulled her to him. Like everything about him, Tom's kisses were intense and passionate. They seemed to come from somewhere deep inside, flowing and spreading until they consumed them both.

Beth allowed herself to fall into the chasm created by his kiss. His masculine scent was intoxicating – a sweet mixture of mint and musk. She inhaled deeply, feeling safe.

After a moment, she felt his lips hesitate against hers. When it seemed that he would pull away, she moved her hands to the side of his face and kissed him hard. Her breasts contracted and expanded with each breath and she pressed them against his chest.

Tom groaned and pulled her closer. Whatever question had been on his mind, or on his lips, disappeared beneath the pressure of her lips. His tongue moved warm and wet against hers and she shuddered from the exquisite contact.

His hands moved along the length of her neck, firm and insistent. She arched against him, giving herself to him completely.

She had taken the lead, and her own lips demanded a response. His lips were soft and full, making his kisses even more passionate. Beth moved into his rhythm, increasing the pace to match her own desire until they were both breathless.

She pulled back for an instant and watched him. His eyes were closed, his cheeks warm and flushed. His thick dark hair was tousled where her fingers had moved through it. Gone was the easy-going smile that appeared so freely onto his lips. Instead, his lips were swollen from her kiss; his expression one of rapture and desire. The picture of him standing so close to her, lost in desire, sent shockwaves through her system. She saw clearly that as much as he filled her with desire, she had a similar effect on him.

She smiled and, as she did, Tom opened his eyes.

"Beth," Tom's own breathing came in short spurts and his heart pounded uncontrollably. The kiss had affected him physically. He had felt all of Beth's passion, but he couldn't help wonder how much of her reaction stemmed from some sort of supernatural chemistry. He was frightened by what he had seen earlier--and intrigued. He wanted to hold her and protect her, and kiss her some more, but something else was interfering. Something bigger than the kiss between them.

Keeping her in the circle of his arms, he asked, "What just happened?"

Beth laughed softly, but her cheeks reddened with guilt and her answer was more like a question. "You kissed me."

Tom turned her to face him. "I'm serious. You were somewhere very far away. I was afraid I couldn't reach you."

Beth's cheeks flamed even further. "Is that why you kissed me?" Her voice turned soft with disappointment and she dropped her gaze.

Tom raised her chin with his index finger. "I kissed you because I wanted to. But, we'll get back to that later. I was worried about you."

His voice belied the concern he felt, but Beth merely smiled. "I was safe."

She knew that now.

"But, what happened?" He wasn't so sure.

Beth struggled to try and explain the knowledge she had gained without words or facts, simply understanding. She looked at Tom with clear eyes. "She was in love with her master."

"Laurilee?" Tom blurted, amazement written all over his face.

Beth nodded.

"How do you know?" Tom struggled to make sense of the happenings around him. He was a writer. He dealt in fantasy for a living. But, this, happening right in front of him, was too much for him to comprehend.

"She told me." Beth, however, was not having the same problem. She spoke in a calm, even tone, as if Laurilee were a real person standing in the room.

"She told you?" Tom practically yelled the word. "Beth, I was standing right here the whole time. I didn't hear anything."

"She wasn't talking to you." Beth's voice was firm, but not sharp.

Tom's head reeled. This was crazy. Trances and dead people. Servants in love with their master. He couldn't even make this kind of stuff up...

He couldn't even make this kind of stuff up...

Maybe he didn't have to.

Tom turned back to Beth, his eyes suddenly bright with interest. "You're saying that we are both standing in a room, this room, and someone talked to you in a manner that I couldn't hear?"

Beth tried gallantly to explain what she didn't fully understand herself. "Talking isn't exactly the right word. It was more like a feeling."

"She touched you?" Tom's voice turned incredulous.

"No." Beth shook her head. "It's more like I felt what she was trying to say. I felt her emotions." Beth nodded this time, more certain of what she was conveying.

"So, you're saying that you felt her feelings?"

Beth nodded. "I think so." Then she nodded again. "Yes."

While she seemed focused on the present, her words sounded soft and dreamy, as if she were still somewhere far away.

"You know she's dead, right?" Tom worked to keep Beth in the present. She seemed to keep drifting off.

Beth's eyebrows furrowed, as if the words were painful, but she nodded. "I know."

"But, you still saw her?" Tom wished he had a pad and paper to take notes.

Beth shook her head immediately. "I felt her." She emphasized the word. "She was sad." Her own expression grew sad as she said the words.

"Because she was in love with her master," Tom prompted, using the only piece of information he had been given.

"Yes." She knit her eyebrows, searching for something or some way to explain. "Something happened. Something very bad. She never recovered."

"What happened?" Tom leaned forward, paying close attention.

Silence for a moment and then Beth shrugged helplessly, "I don't know."

"Do you think he killed her?" Now Tom's writer's instincts were in full gear. He conjured a mental image of scandal and mystery.

But, Beth shook her head. "She left here. For a long, long time. And now she's back."

For a long time, both were silent. Beth concentrated on the past that was slowly slipping from her grip. The smell of lavender left the room, replaced by dust and old tattered garments.

She blinked hard and asked, "Does that sound crazy?"

Her voice had lost the dreamlike quality and she shook her head, holding up a hand. "Don't answer. I know it does."

This time it was Tom's voice that took on a faraway tone. "Actually, it sounds like a mystery or a romance novel. Or something in between."

"What do you mean?" Beth sounded confused.

"I mean," Tom responded, "it doesn't seem real. It sounds like something you'd read in a novel."

Or write in a novel...

"It was real." Beth was adamant. Almost as quickly, she started to doubt herself. "As least I think it was real."

"I believe that you think it was real," Tom cajoled, trying to placate her.

Beth wasn't having any of it. "No. It was real. Laurilee existed and something happened to her. I want to find out what it was."

"Okay." Tom nodded and put his hands on her shoulders. "Let me think about it tonight and see if I can come up with a plan."

Her eyes lit up with hope. "A plan? You would do that for me?"

For her... or for himself... Did it really matter as long as she got the answer she was looking for?

He kissed her lightly on the forehead, wanting to do more, but afraid that the timing was off. "I'll do my best."

As he moved away, she reached for the collar of his shirt and pulled him back to her, smiling, "Now, getting back to that kiss..."

After Tom left the house, Beth sat for a long time in the parlor. She felt safe and warm in the afterglow of Tom's kisses. She closed her eyes and leaned her head against the sofa cushion. She believed, now, that the spirit of Laurilee was in her house. She wasn't afraid. Laurilee needed her help. And she needed Tom.

Tom sat near his laptop late into the evening. Notes and excerpts from his previous story outline lay in scattered sheets atop the metal desk. The remainder of the outline filled the waste basket at his feet. The light bulb that had flashed in his mind earlier grew until it shone like a beacon in his mind. It started with a letter. And a servant in love with her master…

Tom began to type.

Chapter Ten

"Have a great day," Beth called as the last of her guests left for a day of sightseeing.

She smiled at Rosie as the housekeeper gathered the cleaning supplies to begin refreshing the guestrooms. "Looks like it might be a slow day around here."

There were several couples scheduled for the weekend, but that was two days away and she had plenty of time to prepare.

Rosie nodded and headed up the back staircase.

Beth was about to rearrange the kitchen cabinets when the doorbell rang.

Assuming one of the guests had forgotten a key, she hurried to the front door.

She found Tom waiting in the doorway, dangling the keys to his Nova. "I have a plan."

Beth looked at him in disbelief. "You have a plan already?" She looked at her watch. "It's 9:30 in the morning."

"I know. I've been on the phone all morning," he said in excitement. "Now grab your purse. We're driving to Atlanta."

"Atlanta?" Beth choked on the word. "What's in Atlanta?"

"The Georgia Department of Records," Tom replied. "I called in a favor and got us an appointment this afternoon."

He started for the driveway, but Beth stood rooted firmly in the doorway. "This afternoon? Why the rush?"

She looked skeptical and Tom's heart twinged with guilt. The truth was--he needed more information. Last night, in his room, he had taken on something big. A story that revolved around the mystery started here, in Beth's attic. The words flowed onto his computer with ease--the outline almost formed itself. He hadn't felt so alive, so ready for a story, in a long, long time. It was going to be good. He knew it. But, as the story unwound, his natural writer's instincts took over--he needed facts, details to weave into the story-- to make it real. His attention to detail was what set him apart from other writers. To him, this trip was research for a story that would put him back on top of the bestselling list.

He knew that Beth would never understand his reasoning. In a way Tom couldn't understand, Beth had connected with Laurilee--

real or imagined. And she would think Tom was taking advantage if she knew what he was up to. And, if that was true, Tom wasn't ready to face the knowledge. He clung to the fact that once she read the story, Beth would see the value of his idea. He wasn't trying to exploit anyone or anything. He was doing the only job he knew how.

He struggled to look innocent as he replied, "Why not? I thought you wanted to find some answers."

"I do," Beth reluctantly agreed, "but, it just seems kind of odd that all of a sudden you are so gung ho on getting to Atlanta and doing more research. I thought you were just humoring me the other day…" she trailed off, still looking doubtful.

"I was," Tom grinned and then pulled her to him and wrapping his arms around her. "But I also happen to care about you," He spoke softly, kissing the top of her head, inhaling the sweet fragrance of her hair. "And I think that understanding some of the history of this house and the people who lived here that might explain what you're feeling. What is so difficult to understand about that?"

Well, when he put it that way…

Beth felt foolish for being so sensitive. Of course Tom only wanted to help her. He was her friend, after all.

Except that now, as he held her in his arms and she felt the strong muscles of his arms around her shoulders, she wasn't sure if friendship was of interest to her. She felt like she could stay in his arms forever. And when he kissed the top of her head, she moaned softly as her heart swelled. She tilted her head back to look at his face. As he looked down at her, she could feel the sweetness of his breath so close to her lips. That wonderful scent of wintergreen beneath those full lips. Her lips puckered instinctively. She had to kiss him. When he leaned down and touched his lips to hers, she felt the tingling in her insides. His lips were soft against hers, and gentle. The kiss was warm and sweet and left Beth longing for more.

But, Tom pulled away, sighing regretfully. "As much as I would love to stand here and neck with you all day, we do have quite a drive ahead of us."

Beth held up her suddenly empty arms and frowned as he pulled his keys from his pocket. "For someone who is just humoring me, you seem awfully anxious to get to Atlanta."

Tom cleared his throat and refused to meet her eyes. "I hate missing appointments. Especially since this one was last minute… I don't want anyone waiting on us."

Warning bells went off in Beth's head as Tom jabbered just a little too much. He was definitely hiding something. But, for the life of her, Beth couldn't imagine what.

She decided to give in. For now.

"Okay, but we're taking my Jeep. I don't want that rust bucket of yours breaking down on the freeway."

The relief on Tom's face was so obvious that Beth almost laughed. He clearly was not good at hiding his emotions.

He grinned and said, "Did you just insult my car?"

Beth nodded. "I did." She tossed him her keys. "But, as a consolation prize, you can drive."

Once on the highway, Beth tried to maintain a casual air, but she was never very good at hiding her feelings. She turned to Tom, "So, why are you doing this again?"

Tom looked over at her for a second and then turned his attention back to the road. "So you can find out more information on Laurilee."

"I know why I'm going," Beth responded. "Why are you going?"

Tom sighed and said honestly, "So, I can find out more information on Laurilee."

Beth sensed it was the truth, but, try as she might, she couldn't understand why.

"Why do you care?" she pressed.

Tom shrugged, keeping his eyes on the road in front of him. He carefully chose his words to be vague, yet truthful. "I thought about it last night… a lot. The letters and the photo are somehow connected. They were both in the attic. They are both from a period in the distant past. I'm curious, that's all."

Beth studied his profile. By the stiffness in the line of his jaw, she could tell there was more to his answer. She struggled to make sense of his behavior. Tom had, up to now, been one of the most up-front, straightforward people she had ever met. She couldn't make sense of why the subject unnerved him so.

"What do you think the connection is?" she asked, hoping to get him to open up a little more.

Tom was quiet for a while and then he answered, "Obviously, Laurilee, if that's who's in the picture…"

"It was her," Beth interjected, straightening her back defensively.

"Okay," Tom appeased her quickly. "By the picture, Laurilee was clearly a servant of some sort."

Beth nodded in agreement. That sounded reasonable.

"But," Tom continued, "even though the picture was in black and white, the woman in the picture was not a Negro."

"She was mixed blood," Beth agreed immediately.

Tom nodded in agreement. "I think she was an Octoroon--1/8 Negro. Octoroon women were typically known for the combination of their amazing fair skin, hazel eyes and jet black hair. They were considered to be very beautiful."

Beth stroked her own hair. "Yes, she was beautiful."

Tom looked at her oddly, but didn't comment. Instead he continued his commentary. "Many plantation owners, at least the men, preferred to have these women work inside the house because they didn't disgrace the family. They cared for the children, cooked, cleaned and took care of whatever additional needs the family had."

"She was the favored one," Beth said dreamily, looking out the window, a small smile on her face.

"What?" Now Tom openly watched her with suspicion.

Beth didn't notice. She spoke in a thick southern drawl. "There were other servants in the house, but I was the favored one. My place was always secure. The missus... she may not like me much, but I was safe. The master... he'd never let me go."

Tom laughed at her. "Very funny."

"What?" Beth seemed distracted by his statement.

"You were talking in the first person."

"I don't think so." Beth looked at him as if he were crazy.

Tom responded sarcastically, "And I suppose you weren't using a southern accent, either."

"That's right. I wasn't." Beth gave him another confused look and then dismissed his comment with a frown, continuing in her normal voice. "So, Laurilee was the favored servant. Why? Because of James Latte?"

Tom paused for a moment. He would swear she wasn't aware of what she had just said. Either that or she had a very odd sense of humor all of a sudden. But, right now she gazed at him, waiting for his response and he let it go. "More likely because she had some skill... she might have been a terrific seamstress."

"She didn't like to sew," Beth answered absently, not having any idea of where the statement came from, only that it was true. "Anyway, Laurilee said she was safe because the master would never let her go. That would have been James."

"You said that," Tom corrected. "Laurilee is dead."

"So?" She frowned at him, starting to get defensive again. "She was young and beautiful and he was married to Mattie." She made a face. "Why couldn't they fall in love?"

"Because that's not the way things were done back then," Tom reasoned.

"Love doesn't subscribe to traditions," Beth countered. "Maybe that was the problem. They loved each other so deeply, yet they could never be together because of the social implications of their time."

They loved each other so deeply....

The words echoed though her mind, careening through her soul. Beth clutched at her chest as she felt a sharp stab of pain in her heart. She frowned, leaning forward, taking deep slow breaths. Each breath felt like a punch in her sternum.

"Beth?" Tom swerved the car onto the shoulder of the road as Beth slumped forward. "What's wrong?"

He put his hands on her shoulder, feeling utterly helpless. What had come over her? Should he call an ambulance? He'd seen her jerk forward as if in pain and now she sat slumped over as if drained. He pushed on her shoulder a little to rouse her attention. "Are you okay?"

Slowly, she opened her eyes and turned to him. They were red rimmed and her voice shook when she spoke. "She loved him and she could never have him. She knew it. That's why she was so sad."

"Good lord, woman, you scared me to death," Tom exclaimed. "I thought something was really wrong."

Beth felt no shame. "Something was really wrong."

He turned back to her again, his eyes bright with concern. "Beth, you have to stop this. It isn't healthy."

Beth's eyes flared back. "Healthy for whom?"

"For either of us," he scolded and then said sternly, "Laurilee is dead."

Beth felt as if she were being punched in the gut. She answered, her voice high and defensive. "I know Laurilee is dead."

"You sure don't act like it." Tom placed his hands on the steering wheel, but did not pull out onto the street and into traffic flow.

Beth could tell by the line of his jaw that he was struggling to suppress his frustration. Beth watched him and commented, "You're angry."

"I'm not angry," Tom said, but his voice held a different tone. "I'm worried about you. It's not healthy to be so obsessed over this."

Beth's voice grew defensive. "You know, I'm not the only one there. You don't seem to be running from the situation. You're just as curious as I am."

Tom knew she was right. He was curious. But, at least he could separate fact from fiction. He didn't claim to know what Laurilee felt. He just wanted a story. He didn't respond to her comment as he stared forward out onto the highway.

They sat in silence, each lost in their own thoughts.

It was Beth who finally broke the silence. "Tom, I don't want to fight. And I don't want you to be angry." She reached out tentatively to touch the sleeve of his shirt. "I thought you wanted to help me."

"I do want to help you." Tom pursed his lips together for a moment and then said, "I just wish you would stay in the present for one minute. I never know where your head is."

"It's hard for me, too," she admitted. "One minute I'm talking rationally about something that happened in the past and the next minute I'm feeling the heartache of a dead woman." Then she cried out emotionally, "But, what I feel is real. I felt her heartache. In here," she placed a hand on her chest.

"I know you believe that." Tom tried to explain himself without giving way to his true identity. "I'm a man who needs to look at facts. I need to understand things on a concrete level."

"I hear what you're saying," Beth tried to assure him. "But, I can't help it. Some of the things that are happening to me just aren't concrete. I can't explain them, no matter how hard you want me to. I just want to try and understand them."

"So do I," Tom exclaimed, a little too quickly. "I want to understand them. I want to understand you…" He sighed in exasperation.

His words hurt and Beth felt tears prick her eyes. Tom was the most straight-forward, down-to-earth person she had ever met. He lived a simple, honest life. She was a nuisance to him and he was too kind to tell her so.

"I'm not so hard to understand…" she began and then let her voice trail off. What difference did it make? The bottom line was that he didn't want to have to deal with her or her crazy ideas. She was disrupting his simple life and he was probably anxious to solve the mystery of Laurilee so that he could be done with her.

Tom watched the disappointment in her eyes and mentally kicked himself. He hadn't wanted to hurt her feelings. Beth wasn't hard to understand. It was himself. He was leading a double life. Caught between the fantasy world that earned his salary and the real world that was increasingly revolving around Beth. He couldn't live with himself knowing he caused her pain. He would just tell her the truth. He would just tell her.

"Beth," he began, "there's something…"

And then he met her eyes. They were huge and liquid, gazing at him as if touching his very soul. And her lips, swollen in a pout, were vulnerable and sexy at the same time. Her cheeks flushed under his blatant stare.

He felt guilt and shame and then desire.

He pulled her to him, crushing her against him. His lips moved against hers, forcing them to respond. When they parted slightly, he thrust his tongue between them, tasting her and savoring the sweetness of her mouth.

Beth felt liquid fire rush through her body. Tom's kiss was rough, raw with desire. All rationality left her mind as she moved with him, clinging desperately to the ride his lips charged against her mouth. He was reckless and wild and she pulled him even closer, lost in the waves of shock and pleasure.

When he pulled away, they were both breathing rapidly, chests heaving, cheeks flushed. Tom laid a hand on Beth's cheek, feeling its heat. His voice was raspy with desire as he said, "See? You're not hard to understand at all, Beth." He put his other hand on her other cheek. "You're easy to understand."

Tom sat back against the seat and put his hands on the steering wheel. As much as he enjoyed kissing Beth, he was disappointed in his own weakness. He had lost his opportunity to come clean. Or maybe he hadn't wanted to take the opportunity in the first place.

Beth didn't notice his dilemma. She was caught up in her own feelings. Her attraction to Tom was undeniable. She trusted him and felt safe with him. At the same time, he didn't understand the depth of her connection to Laurilee. Somehow, in a way she didn't understand, Laurilee was tied to her. She couldn't just let it go. She had to find out the truth.

She turned to Tom now and said quietly, "Nothing is easy."

He looked at her and nodded. "Maybe you're right."

"Let's just concentrate on the things we can control," she suggested.

"Okay," he agreed, reached over and taking her hand as he pulled back onto the highway. Wrapping her fingers around his, they sat hand-in-hand throughout the remainder of the drive.

Atlanta brought back a wave of nostalgia to Beth. The most she had seen of the city of her childhood in the past five years was the inside of the airport and the freeway heading out of town. The city had grown tremendously. Bright strip centers occupied space that had once been rolling pastures. Several new high rise buildings lined the skyline. Traffic bustled in the heat of the early afternoon.

Tom maneuvered the Jeep expertly through the traffic. Within minutes, they were parked outside the State Archives and Records Building in downtown Atlanta.

"Are you ready?" He looked at her with a grin.

Beth nodded and they went inside. Her eyes widened at the massive interior with its many rooms and doorways.

"It's huge in here," she breathed, speaking in a whisper as one would do in a library.

"I read on the website that inside this building are over 100,000 cubic feet of records and over 65,000 reels of microfilm."

"How will we ever find what we need?" Beth couldn't imagine trying to sort through that amount of information.

"I took the liberty of asking my contact here to pull some files for us," Tom admitted grandly. "Here we are now."

He ushered her into a door marked PRIVATE. Inside was a back office full of cubicles and administrative staff. Tom hesitated for a moment and then touched her arm softly. "Wait here for just a second."

Beth stood in the doorway as Tom approached a woman sitting at a desk just to their right. He offered his hand and spoke in hushed tones to the woman. Beth watched as the woman jumped to her feet and shook Tom's hand with enthusiasm. Her round face grew animated and her hands moved about excitedly as she spoke. She handed Tom something Beth couldn't identify and he nodded and smiled.

Amazing. Beth's own expression grew dumfounded at the exchange. What could possibly be so exciting about the State Archives? And so secret that she had to be banished to the doorway? A seed of irritation settled in Beth's stomach.

She moved forward, clearing her throat, and headed toward the conspirators. Tom jerked upright and spoke before Beth could introduce herself. "I think we are ready here."

The large-hipped woman led them; or rather lead Tom while Beth followed behind, to a cubicle in the back of the room, where a microfilm reader and several transparencies were stacked neatly. Beth was not introduced, nor acknowledged. Instead, the woman smiled at Tom as if he were the King of England. Beth trailed behind, sulking.

After showing Tom how to work the machine, the woman stepped aside, still beaming in Tom's direction. Beth, obviously, didn't exist. "It was such a pleasure to meet you," she gushed, pumping Tom's hand up and down in a vigorous handshake. "If you need anything…"

"We'll let you know," Tom assured her, waiting patiently until the woman made her way to the front of the room before turning back to Beth and the microfilm.

"What was that all about?" Beth asked, feeling something akin to jealousy taking hold in the pit in her stomach. Although the clerk had more of a grandmotherly air about her than that of a scheming vixen, Beth wasn't sure she liked all that gushing… and handshaking. It was too close to hand holding and that was her territory.

Tom laughed at her. "I just have that effect on women."

Beth was not amused. She harrumphed loudly and in her most distinct British accent and sat down at the table.

Still laughing, Tom took the seat next to her. "Let's see what we have here."

He started loading the first transparency. Tiny print filled the small square screen and Tom began scrolling down the tinted computer screen.

Beth, however, wasn't quite finished. She sat back in her seat and folded her arms across her chest, asking pointedly, "Did you know her from somewhere?"

"Who? Dora?" Tom asked, not looking up from the screen. "No, I've never met her before."

Beth harrumphed again, a little louder, and then asked, "Then why was she so friendly?"

Tom shrugged, trying to appear nonchalant, but wishing Beth would let the subject drop. "She probably doesn't get that many visitors back here." Especially ones who just happen to be her favorite author, he added silently, hating himself for the secrets he kept.

"It still seems weird," Beth muttered, as she glanced halfheartedly at the screen.

Luckily at that moment, the records of James Latte filled the screen and Beth pushed aside any thoughts of the clerk as she leaned forward to read the information. Birth Certificate. Marriage Certificate. Death Certificate. To Beth, the date of James Latte's death stood out: 1875.

"He was awfully young," she commented. "Does it list a cause of death?"

Tom clicked on the screen, enlarging the death certificate.

"Says here: heart failure." Tom pointed at the wording on the certificate.

"Doesn't that seem odd?" Beth questioned. "He was young and strong. He spent his days working on a cotton plantation. And, after all that, to have a weak heart."

Tom shrugged. "Some things can't be explained. You know what they say, truth is stranger than fiction."

Beth snorted, "Not some of the fiction I've seen in book stores lately. Seems like the subject matter is getting more outrageous by the moment."

Tom winced. Her words struck awfully close to home. He tried to make light of the subject. "Not a fan of popular fiction, I take it?"

"Not really," Beth answered. "I like historical novels, where you can actually learn something as you read."

"And the woman always gets her man?" Tom couldn't resist goading her just a little.

Beth turned to him with raised eyebrows, a touch of fire glowing in her eyes and sass on her lips. "Is there something wrong with that?"

"Nope," Tom shook his head quickly. "It's just that in those stories the man is always a beast right up until the woman straightens him out and they live happily after."

"And your point is?" Beth smirked, keeping her eyebrows raised.

Tom closed his eyes and laughed. "My point is… not all men are beasts."

"Really?" she drew out the word as if what she was hearing was new information to her.

"Yes, really." Tom leaned towards her, forgetting about the computer screen in front of him. He moved his face close to hers. "Am I a beast?"

Beth felt his warm breath against her lips. Her heart rate escalated and she struggled to keep herself from sighing aloud. The scent of him swirled around her making her dizzy. He was so close to her that if she moved forward even a fraction, their foreheads would touch. Or their noses… Or their lips…

Exhaling slowly, she answered properly, "I don't know you well enough to make that judgment."

"I think you do," Tom whispered, closing the gap between them.

The kiss was slow and sweet, just like Tom. He never seemed impatient or rushed. He savored the touch, feeling his way over her lips and into her mouth with his tongue. Her own body felt alive with desire. She wanted to throw him onto the table and tear off his clothes.

Appalled and aroused at the same time, Beth let her imagination run wild. Yes, she would swipe away the computer monitor and place her hands against his chest and push him backwards at the same time, ripping off the buttons on his shirt. And then she would stand over him, admiring the dark, soft hair on his chest covering his rippled muscles as he gazed up at her.

While he lay helpless before her, she would swing her long hair across his chest, letting her thick curls trail along his stomach where she would press her cheek against his hot flesh. And then, when she was ready, she would press her lips to his and there would be nothing slow or sweet about it.

"Oh my," Beth breathed the words as Tom's hands tangled in her hair, gently pulled her away and gazed at her.

His smile was lazy and his voice deep and sexy as he said, "See? I'm not a beast at all."

Beth sighed deeply and said almost inaudibly, "No, but I am."

Tom frowned at her and she smiled innocently. "Never mind."

The moment was broken, but the promise of later lingered in the air.

As they turned back to the computer, they sat closer together, shoulders touching and the air of intimacy that had been missing earlier was now distinctly present.

They scrolled quickly through the information listed on the screen. Although the amount of historical facts was intriguing, both

Tom and Beth had only one thing on their mind. Finding out who Laurilee was.

After about an hour, Beth leaned back, rubbing her temples. "How can you stare at that thing so intently? I have dots dancing in front of my eyelids," she grumbled.

Tom leaned over and placed a kiss on Beth's forehead. "Don't worry. Something will turn up soon."

"I hope so." Beth sat up, sounding dejected.

"Don't worry," Tom repeated, sounding confident. In doing research for his novels, he quite often spent hours on end in front of a screen just like this one. His books, while sometimes bizarre in content, were fiercely accurate. He was a stickler for details and he would not let a subject drop until he had all of the answers.

In the blur of information, something caught his eye. "Look at this." Tom switched film and began scrolling again. "It's James Latte's account book."

"What kind of accounts?" Beth leaned in and took a closer look. It was a ledger, writing in longhand that consisted of a list of... "People?" Beth breathed the word in awe.

"Slaves," Tom whispered, struggling to read the expansive writing of the time period.

Beth held her breath as Tom scrolled down the page. There were so many names. Her heart pounded heavily as, one by one, the names rolled by. It was a huge piece of history and it overwhelmed her slightly. But, the name they were looking for overwhelmed her the most. Laurilee. They had no other reference. Only the name that Beth heard whispered in the night and saw signed on the bottom of a love letter.

Beth started to panic as the pages rolled by. She grabbed Tom's sleeve. "What if she's not there?"

Beth closed her eyes, suddenly afraid to look. It felt like her last chance. If Laurilee wasn't listed in these records, maybe she didn't exist. Maybe Beth was crazy.

"Hold on," Tom cautioned, tapping on the space bar. A second later, he exclaimed, "Here. Look."

Beth pried her eyes open. In an instant, it was there before her.

Laurilee Williams.
Slave.
Purchased 1859.

"She was real," Beth choked, feeling her breath catch in her throat. "She was real."

Beth's eyes fluttered shut as the words danced before her and she slumped forward into Tom's arms.

Chapter Eleven

"Beth."

Tom's voice came from inside the fuzz in her brain and Beth opened her eyes. She lay nestled in Tom's arms where she had collapsed in a rush of emotion.

She stared at Tom in awe and whispered the words floating through her mind over and over again. "She was real."

"It appears so," Tom agreed, holding her for a moment longer before turning back to the ledger.

"Look her up," Beth urged, her voice barely more than a choked whisper.

They did. She had been born in 1845.

"She was fourteen when she was purchased," Beth said, doing the math quickly in her head.

She died in 1881, at the age of 35.

"She was so young." Beth felt sadness well up in her chest at the thought. "Do you think she died some mysterious death at the plantation? Is that why she can't leave?"

"No," Tom said, pointing at a particular spot on the screen. "She died in Atlanta. She must have left the plantation."

"Do you think she was given her freedom?" Beth asked.

"I don't know," Tom said. "The house servants, when they got too old to be of use, were almost always removed from the house; and, I suppose in some rare instances, especially if they were of mixed blood, slaves were freed from their indenture."

They scrolled through the files for another hour, but found no further information of relevance. Laurilee's name produced little more than a record of her birth and death. Personal information on slaves was not considered important enough to track at the time.

Beth sat back in dejection. "We really haven't learned anything."

"Except that Laurilee was indeed a slave that worked on the Latte Plantation," Tom pointed out. "That is pretty significant, I think."

"There's more," Beth persisted, nonplussed. "What does she want? And why did she pick me?"

"The only thing we didn't check was the listing of non-governmental items." Tom maneuvered to the correct microfilm.

"There might be some family letters or photographs. The state saves things that they consider to have cultural or historical value."

There wasn't much.

A copy of the family photograph Beth and Tom had seen in the published book. Two or three letters written in fancy script from Mattie's mother.

"Remember, Mattie had all the money," Tom noted when Beth commented on the lack of information about James' side of the family.

Beth squinted at the elaborate writing. "I can barely make out the words."

"There was a great deal of local gossip; apparently the fall social season was in full swing. Beth read aloud, squinting over the words, "…now, I don't want to upset you dear, but your sister, Cassandra, is with child once more. However, you mustn't hold that against her. It's not her fault that you are unable to bear children…"

"Unable to bear children?" Tom and Beth exclaimed the words at the exact same time, turning to face each other.

"What is the date on the letter?" Beth asked, excitement in her voice.

They scrolled back to the top of the page. October 6, 1860.

"But, she had children," Beth puzzled. Jonathon and Samantha.

"We saw them in the pictures. We haven't found any proof that Mattie was their mother," Tom pointed out.

"But…" Beth started and then stopped. She raised a hand to her lips. "No. Tom do you think?"

Tom shrugged. "Stranger things have happened."

He looked up another name. Jonathon Latte.

At first the information appeared useless. Birth Certificate. Marriage Certificate. Death Certificate. All in perfect order.

Tom enlarged the document bearing Jonathon's birth information and read aloud. "Born: April, 28, 1861 at Midtown Hospital in Atlanta. Weight: 6 lbs, 8 oz. Father: James Latte. Mother:…"

Tom stopped reading. Beth, who had been following along with her eyes, gasped. "Oh, Tom."

Tom took a deep breath and read on, "Mother: Laurilee Williams."

Although they both knew the outcome, they looked up Samantha Latte and found the same information. Born August 2, 1864. Father: James Latte. Mother: Laurilee Williams.

Beth raised a shaking hand to her lips. "Those were Laurilee's children."

Tom nodded his head in agreement.

"I was right," she exclaimed, looking at Tom. "She and James were in love. They had children together."

Tom hated to burst her bubble, but felt inclined to point out the obvious. "Children that were raised by James and Mattie."

"I know. It doesn't make sense," Beth said, closing her eyes, searching somewhere inside herself for the place that Laurilee occupied. "Laurilee loved her children." She felt that in her heart and believed it.

She turned to Tom with huge questioning eyes. "How could she give up her children?"

Tom locked his soft grey eyes with hers, trying to make sense of the situation. "I'm sure it happened quite often in those days."

Beth felt her breath quicken. Panic started to well up inside her as she cried, "Not to Laurilee. She loved her children. She didn't want to give them up."

"During that time, if she was a slave, her children were as much property of the owner as Laurilee herself." Tom saw Beth moving to the brink of another spell. Her eyes scanned the room wildly, almost as if her own children were missing. He knew that she had some link to this particular past, even if he couldn't logically explain it. He struggled to keep things in perspective. Talking gently, he told her, "Beth, you have to remain calm. This happened a long time ago."

"No," Beth shook her head violently, also struggling to remain in the present. "It's happening now. I can feel it. Here." She pounded her chest and stared at him. "Can't you understand that?"

But, he couldn't. He was a writer. Situations like this occurred in his imagination. They weren't real. They were pieces of a puzzle in his head. The beginnings of a novel. Slowly, some of the pieces started to fit together, creating an image. As more and more of the pieces came together, the story began to unfold. And then, it was a matter of finding the additional information and putting things in the right spot to complete the novel.

But, it wasn't real.

At least not to him.

Beth, on the other hand, felt as if she were living in the past. Her heart pounded in her chest. She felt short of breath, as if she had been running for a long time. She felt a panic that she couldn't explain. As if her heart were being torn from inside.

Clutching her chest, Beth lowered her head and closed her eyes.

She felt as if… well, as if her own children were being taken from her.

She stopped and took several deep breaths, trying to regain her composure. Trying to remain in the present. She was Beth Willis. She didn't have children. She had no idea what losing children would feel like.

She wanted to go home and talk to Laurilee. Laurilee had all the answers.

Even as the thought formed in her mind, she knew it sounded crazy. Laurilee was dead. She had died over a hundred years ago. She couldn't talk. She didn't have the answers.

Because she didn't exist.

She did exist.

Beth opened her eyes and looked at the screen before her. Her name, Laurilee Williams, stood out like a spotlight.

She did exist.

And she'd had her children taken away from her.

She turned to Tom. "Let's go home."

As they walked through the parking lot, Tom noticed how quiet she was. He asked softly, "Are you sure you're okay?"

Beth nodded. She felt calmer now. It seemed as though she reacted to each new piece of information just as Laurilee would and then it took several minutes, sometimes even hours, to recover her own composure. Smiling sadly, she said, "I came here hoping to find answers and now I have even more questions."

Tom nodded. "Sometimes information is dangerous."

To Tom, information was another piece of the puzzle. But he knew to Beth it was much more than that. He softened his tone and touched her arm gently. "The answers will come."

Beth, for her part, wasn't so sure. That was up to Laurilee.

As they wound their way back to Garden Ridge, Beth felt some of the tension leave her shoulders. She hadn't realized how much thinking about Laurilee took out of her. It really did feel as if she lost control of her body for a time, as impossible as that sounded.

She felt as if hours had passed. In fact, she couldn't remember if they had eaten lunch or not. On cue, her stomach growled.

Turning to Tom, she asked, "Can we stop to eat? I'm starved."

They found a roadside diner, the kind that catered to weary travelers, complete with a gift shop. The little restaurant suited Beth. Even though the trip lasted only a day, she felt weary down to her bones.

They ate quickly, with little conversation.

As Tom took care of the bill, Beth wandered through the tiny gift shop. They stocked all of the usual items: t-shirts, ashtrays and a variety of items carrying a Georgia emblem. A rack of postcards. A shelf of magazines. Assorted paperback novels.

Beth spun the round rack of novels. Most of them were quite dated. She saw quite a few suspense titles and made a face. She preferred romance novels where the heroine met the man of her dreams and ended up living happily ever after. One book caught her eye and she reached out to remove it from the bin. The Cemetery. The cover depicted an eerie graveyard with one skeletal hand sticking out from a gravesite. Beth shivered at the realistic cover and then turned the book over, skimming over the synopsis on the back.

It was a ghost story, full of creatures from the dead, complete with blood and gore. Beth shivered again. How gruesome.

What kind of person wrote such stories?

She turned back to the front cover. Sam Shelling.

The cover touted him as "America's #1 ghost writer". Thinking back, she had heard the name before and she thought several of his books had been made into movies. He was quite famous, although she had never read any of his writing.

Out of curiosity more than anything, Beth flipped to the inside back cover, looking for a picture of the author.

She expected to see a large man with thick glasses and an intense stare.

What she found was a picture of Tom.

"No. It can't be." Beth raised a hand to her mouth, dropping the book in the process. It clattered loudly to the floor and she picked it up quickly.

She stared at the picture. There was no mistake. Tom was Sam Shelling.

"Tom," she whispered aloud, looking around the store for him.

He was not at the counter. Beth rushed forward and paid for the book quickly. She didn't want this to turn into another figment of her imagination.

Purchase in hand, she waited by the car for Tom. Each second that passed turned her shock into fury.

By the time he strolled casually out the door, she was livid.

"Ready to go?" he called out cheerfully, tossing the keys into the air and catching them lightly.

"I don't think so," she said. She was not about to get in the car with someone who had suddenly become a stranger.

Tom frowned at her, obviously confused. "Did you want desert or something?"

"No, Tom, I don't want desert," she spat the words at him. "Or should I call you Sam?"

Tom stopped. The look on his face told its own story. Beth read his expression and sucked in a loud, audible breath. It was true. That look was all the confirmation she needed. She waited for the denial. The explanation. Anything.

But, after a second, he replied evenly, "My name is Tom. You can call me that."

She shook her head. Ripping the book from its paper bag, she threw it at him. "What about this?"

The book bounced off his shoulder and skittered to the ground. Tom didn't take his eyes off Beth. He felt as if his own insides were being wrenched from him. He had known that he was taking a risk not telling her the truth. Now he had to pay the consequences.

"You lied to me," Beth accused, watching him with large, luminous eyes. Although her jaw was set as if in stone, her eyes betrayed the hurt she felt.

"Beth," Tom took a step toward her. He wanted to take her in his arms and explain everything. He hadn't meant to hurt her. He was protecting himself; that was all. He cared so much for her. He would never hurt her.

But the words wouldn't come.

She backed away from his touch, repeating, "You lied."

He took a deep breath and said, "I know. I'm sorry."

Beth shook her head. "I don't understand. What are you hiding?"

"Myself," Tom stated emphatically. "I moved to Garden Ridge to escape Sam Shelling. In Garden Ridge, I'm Tom Hartman, librarian. No recognition. No questions." No pressure. "That's how I want it to be."

"But, we're friends," Beth protested. "You should have told me."

"Maybe," Tom agreed. "But, I wanted you to know me as myself, not as Sam Shelling."

Beth laughed ruefully, "I don't even know who Sam Shelling is."

Tom cocked an eyebrow in disbelief and Beth was forced to admit, "Okay, maybe I've heard the name before."

"Look," Tom began again. "I'm sorry. I was wrong not to tell you, but it had nothing to do with you. It's about me. Can't we still be friends?"

Beth stared at him for a long moment and then glared at him with just a touch of glimmer in her eye. "Are you going to lie to me anymore?"

Tom felt a twinge in his gut, but he pushed it away. She was close to forgiving him and he wasn't going to blow it now. He'd have to think of another way to tell her about his current project. "I sure hope not. That's some power you have in that arm." He rubbed his shoulder where the paperback had bounced off him. "I'll probably have a bruise."

Beth stooped down and snatched the paperback off the ground, sliding it into her purse before getting in the car.

As they got in the car, Tom reached into the back seat and pulled out a manila folder. "I guess now that the cat is out of the bag, I can give you this."

Beth opened the folder and exclaimed, "It's a printout of all the information on the Latte's." She turned to Tom. "How did you get that?"

Tom had the grace to blush. "Remember Dora that you were so jealous of?"

"I was not jealous…" Beth started and then snapped her jaw shut. "Let me guess… Dora is a big fan of Sam Shellings?"

"President of the Atlanta fan club."

Tom grinned. Beth shook her head. "Now, I feel stupid."

Tom replied seriously, "Don't feel stupid, Beth. You didn't know."

"Thanks to you."

She flipped through the pages. Re-reading the letters to Malthilde, Beth racked her brain to figure out what made Laurilee give up her children. Her mind grew fuzzy as she pictured Laurilee pregnant and alone…

Laurilee had been banished to her room in the attic while the Mister and Missus talked. After what seemed like an eternity, the couple opened the door to her room.

Upon seeing the Mistress of the house, Laurilee scurried back to cower in the corner. With eyes full of distaste, the lady approached and towered over the crouched girl. Laurilee glanced around wildly, looking for some sign of encouragement. James, however, remained in the corner, unable to meet her eye.

"Laurilee," the woman spoke, her deep masculine voice creeping across the girl's skin. "I am appalled at your behavior. You have disgraced yourself and your family."

Laurilee dropped her eyes, hoping that her family wouldn't suffer because of her behavior. They were good people and they needed the work.

"But, I'm going to save you," the woman continued in her haughty voice, "I'm going to raise your child as my own."

Laurilee raised her eyes in shock, trying to understand what was being said.

The woman nodded. "I have always wanted children, but have been unable to conceive. This will present a perfect opportunity."

Still Laurilee stared, not comprehending.

Mrs. Latte snorted in disgust at Laurilee's ignorance. She explained curtly, "It's perfectly simple. You will stay here, in the attic, until such time as your baby is born. Meanwhile, I'll start wearing a pillow beneath my corset. No one will suspect a thing." She smiled over her shoulder at her husband. "We'll send out the announcements tomorrow."

James Latte swallowed and nodded.

"And you," Mattie swung back in the girl's direction. "I don't want to see or hear a peep from this room. I'll tell the other servants you've gone to help my sister for a while. Have I made myself clear?"

Laurilee nodded, although she didn't understand at all...

Beth awoke with a start and a gasp. She sat straight up in her seat, staring out at the landscape passing by.

Tom gave her a sideways glance. "Have a nice nap?"

"She didn't know." Beth placed a shaking hand on her forehead and repeated. "She didn't understand."

"Who didn't know?" Tom asked and then said, "Laurilee?"

Beth nodded. "I had a dream. She got pregnant and Mattie took the baby. She didn't understand what was happening. They locked her in the attic and then took her baby as soon as it was born. Mattie pretended all along to be pregnant." Beth blinked back tears of emotion. "Laurilee watched from the window as they christened the baby boy Jonathon Latte in the garden. She thought James was going to take care of her and bring her babies back, but he didn't. She never understood what happened"

For once, Tom didn't question the validity of Beth's dream. He didn't understand it, but he knew that whatever Beth felt was real. So, he said softly, "How sad."

"It's horrible," Beth stated with emotion. "How could someone do that?" She turned her head and placed her forehead against the glass and murmured, "It's just not right."

"You know, those were different times," Tom ventured quietly. "Do you think that maybe Laurilee was glad that her children were afforded opportunities that she could have never provided?"

Beth closed her eyes again, trying to bring back the images in her head.

After a moment, she shook her head, "All I can see from Laurilee is sadness."

Chapter Twelve

Two days later, Beth leaned against the doorway of the library's parlor, listening to the end of story time.

Knowing that Tom was Sam Shelling revealed him in a new light to her. Suddenly, she was amazed that everyone couldn't see how special he was. This was no ordinary person. He had a shine. He was a celebrity.

Story time at the library was an event hosted and starred in by Tom. She could see the animation in his gestures as he told the story. The sparkle in his eyes. The articulation of his voice. It was like watching a play. Unlike most libraries, story time in Garden Ridge did not consist of picking a book and reading it aloud. Each week's tale was an original Tom Hartman masterpiece. Sam Shelling might be the master of the suspense novel, but Tom Hartman told a pretty captivating tale in his own right.

The children leaned forward eagerly as Tom told a wonderful story about an octopus living in the ocean world. It was the stuff Disney movies were made of.

Beth was impressed and proud at the same time.

She smiled as the children clapped and hollered when the octopus was reunited with his underwater family and lived happily ever after. Pleased with his ending, Tom accepted the exuberant hugs and high fives from the children as well as the grateful thanks of the parents who promised to bring their children back next week.

As the last of the children went flying down the front sidewalk, Beth grinned at Tom, who was straightening the discarded chairs and mats. "That was some story."

Tom nodded. "Baboo the octopus is quite the little dickens." Baboo had been the center of several of Tom's stories and the regulars to story time were familiar with his antics.

"How come you don't write children's stories?" Beth asked seriously. He was really good at it.

Tom just shrugged and continued his cleaning.

Beth nodded and then said casually, "I read your book."

Tom stopped, his back to her, and stood silently for a split second and then turned to face her. His face was carefully neutral, but she could see the interest in his eyes as he responded, "Really?"

Beth nodded.

He watched her for a moment and then asked, "What did you think?"

She tilted her head to one side. "I didn't know you had such a vivid imagination."

Tom raised a disbelieving eyebrow in her direction and she laughed, "Okay, maybe I suspected it…"

Then she looked at him with a serious expression. "It seemed really out of your nature to me."

Tom didn't meet her eyes. "What do you mean?"

"You know what I mean," she prompted. "The gore and the suspense – it was a scary book. I didn't know you had such a dark side."

"It was just a book," Tom responded defensively.

"Okay," Beth held up her hands and Tom instantly backed down.

"I'm sorry," he said. "But, you need to understand. That's what I do. I write ghost stories. I'm not a monster. Just a writer."

His tone sounded self-deprecating, which Beth found a little disconcerting, considering his status in his profession. She challenged him, saying, "A famous writer."

"Maybe not." Tom's tone changed and she could hear a certain frustration in his voice. "You're only as famous as your last book."

She could see that he was upset and suddenly she thought she understood why.

"And it's been awhile since your last book?" Beth guessed correctly.

Tom nodded without answering. His eyes went dark and brooding.

There was silence for a moment while Beth digested this new information. Then she turned to Tom. "Why don't you just write a new book?"

"If only it were that easy," Tom said. "I've had writer's block for the last two years. That's another reason I didn't want my identity revealed. There's been a lot of pressure for me to release a new book. I started some things, but nothing really took shape. I was waiting for something special."

She caught the inflection in his tone. "And did you find it?"

He shrugged, averting his gaze. "Maybe."

"So, you're working on something now?" Beth was encouraged by that. She hated to see Tom's spirits down.

Tom was vague in his answer. "It's just an idea."

But, she'd seen the spark in his eye. "It's a good idea, though, isn't it?"

Tom nodded, but his expression still seemed guarded. "I think so."

"You think so?" Beth teased, trying to lift his spirits. "That's not the Tom Hartman I know. I'll bet it's a great idea."

But, Tom back-peddled, still not wanting to meet her eyes. "Let's not talk about it right now." He wasn't far enough along with the book to show it to her. He wanted it to be perfect so that she would see how special the story was. He desperately wanted to change the subject.

But, she continued to press. "Why not?" Beth wanted to know. "Is it a ghost story? Are you afraid I won't like it?"

Her words were playful, but Tom recoiled as if struck.

Beth stopped, her smile fading. That was exactly it. She took a deep breath and asked carefully, "Why wouldn't I like it?"

Tom paced away from her like a caged animal, trying to escape. "You will like it. You have to like it."

The desperation in his voice caused alarm bells to sound in Beth's head. She couldn't imagine herself not liking anything about Tom. She didn't necessarily like ghost stories, but, if they were Tom's, they would be fine. What could be so bad that she wouldn't approve? Unless it was about her. Or someone she cared about.

And then she knew.

She walked up to him, grabbed his shoulder, and turned him to face her. "It's Laurilee, isn't it? That's why you've been so interested in her."

Tom didn't meet her gaze. "It's just an idea."

"But, it's an idea about Laurilee, right?" she pressed.

He rubbed his fingertips across his temple in a gesture that was part anger, part distress, but mostly in relief. It was sooner than he would have liked, but now that the truth was out, he could explain everything and she would understand. He nodded and looked at her. "Yes, Beth, it is."

He started to explain, "It's just an outline, but it feels right." It was a little understated; he was, in fact, over half way through the first draft. The words seemed to pour forth effortlessly. All he needed was the ending.

"No."

The vehemence in Beth's voice startled Tom away from his thoughts. He stared at her and asked, "What do you mean-- no?"

Beth met his gaze with steely eyes. The image of his book cover lingered clearly in her mind. "You can't exploit her like that."

"I'm not going to exploit her," he protested.

"That's what you do," she countered. "I read your book. You write about freaks and goblins. Laurilee is a person…" Beth trailed off, knowing that Laurilee was, in fact, a ghost which was what, in fact, Sam Shelling wrote about. "You just can't do it."

"Beth, I know how you feel about Laurilee. And it's not like that. This book will be different. I promise." Tom used all of his persuasive powers to try and make her soften. The rest of his career hinged on this book. He felt it in his gut. It was going to change his life.

At the same time, Beth had changed his life as well. She brought light and happiness. He didn't want to lose her. But, he couldn't give up the book. Even if he wanted to, Sam Shelling would never allow it – it was part of Sam and Sam was part of Tom. The struggle showed on his face as he asked earnestly, "Will you at least give it a chance?"

Beth shook her head, amazed and ashamed to find that she was crying. The deeper implications of their prior conversations were making their way into her heart. "You took advantage of me. You used my vulnerability to gather information about your book."

"That's not true," he exclaimed. But, he knew, in his heart, that she was at least partially correct.

Beth knew it as well. She looked at him with sadness in her eyes. "You are not the person I thought you were."

"Beth," Tom's heart broke at her words and the sad resolution on her face. "Don't do this. I'm sorry."

"You might be," she acknowledged, "but Sam Shelling isn't." It was a huge admission on her part. She didn't know Sam Shelling, but she didn't like him. And she couldn't have Tom without him.

Tom stood, open mouthed, as she turned to walk away. Her words were more insightful than she could have imagined because Sam Shelling already wanted to go back inside and work on the book. It was Tom's heart that was breaking. Sam Shelling didn't have a heart.

"Beth, please…"

Beth shook her head, preventing him from completing his sentence. She didn't turn around. She opened the front door and walked down the porch stairs to the front walkway. Her back was stiff and straight. She did not slow down.

"Beth," he called again, his voice rising in panic. He had to keep her near him. To make her understand. "I love you."

She stopped, stood still for a moment and then swung around to face him. Large tears stood out in her blue eyes. "How dare you say that to me now?"

"It's the truth," Tom said softly. And as he stood there, looking at her, he knew it was true.

But, Beth didn't buy it for a second. "You don't know what the truth is," she replied, as the tears spilled over her eyelashes.

For the second time, she turned her back and walked away. Tom stood helplessly, watching her retreating form. He stood for a moment, or an hour, he wasn't sure which, until darkness settled in. Finally, he turned and walked up the pathway to his house.

The blinking light from his computer welcomed him like an old friend.

Beth spent the next week walking around in a fog. Her guests checked in and checked out with her barely recognizing the names. Luckily, Rosie filled the gap effortlessly, cooking the meals and keeping the guests comfortable. She asked no questions when Beth's private line rang unanswered or the doorbell resounded through the house with no response. She did not comment on the growing circles beneath Beth's eyes or the gaunt lines in her face; only placed a cup of tea next to the morning paper when Beth arose.

There were no complaints of noise in the courtyard that week, but Beth felt Laurilee's presence watching over her as she spent hours a day shivering beneath the thick quilt on her bed. She tried to communicate with Laurilee; however to offer comfort or receive it – she didn't know, but Laurilee kept a distance.

The letters were read and reread by Beth; sometimes in bed; sometimes from a wicker chair in the courtyard; sometimes from the attic room where Laurilee spent so much of her lifetime. Beth looked for clues; for hidden meanings in the words; but, she found no answers.

One night later in the week, Beth sat in the parlor with several of her guests watching TV. It was a prime time news show with a very famous anchor. Beth had tuned out most of the show, remaining in the parlor mostly for appearances' sake, when one of the stories suddenly caught her attention.

It was a story about a paranormal research society based out of Colorado. This group of people used advanced technical equipment to record paranormal activity in all sorts of locations. Beth sat forward and watched the segment with interest. They discussed the detailed procedures used to track and gather information. They were quick to point out that research into the paranormal was not a science; it was a theory at best. But, these people took the information seriously and believed in what they were doing. At the end of the show, Beth wrote down the phone number and tucked it into her pocket.

The next morning, based on a reference from the organization featured on the show, Beth found herself speaking with a local research group in Atlanta.

The person on the phone asked brief questions about her situation and seemed professional and genuinely interested. After Beth gave a brief description of the incidents in her house, the woman followed up with more specific questions. Beth felt more comfortable as the woman took her answers seriously and asked relevant questions. Finally, someone seemed to believe what she was feeling.

"Where have the appearances occurred? Have they been at specific times or intervals?"

Beth thought for a moment. "Mostly in the attic and in my room," she noted, "oh, and the courtyard," she added, thinking of the children. "But, at no specific times."

"Were the occurrences visual or auditory?"

"Both," Beth replied. "I've heard Laurilee's voice and I've seen her in the attic and in the window of my room. I haven't heard the children's voices, but several of my guests have."

There was a pause, presumably as the woman took notes, and then she asked, "You mention the word Laurilee. Do you know the identity of the apparition?"

"Yes," Beth said. "Laurilee Williams. She was a slave that lived in the house in 1859. I have a picture of her."

"And the children?"

Beth shook her head. "I'm not sure. I think they were Laurilee's. I have pictures of them as well."

"Ms. Willis," the woman continued, "what is the purpose for contacting this office?"

"Laurilee wants something from me. I want to find out what. Can you help me?"

For the first time, the woman did not sound encouraging. "We can conduct a survey of the house, noting any cold spots or energy sources. We can take photographs, but because of the random nature of the activity, it's unlikely that any activity will be captured on film or otherwise. Usually our services consist of performing the extensive background research on the resident to corroborate any paranormal activity a person might be experiences, but it sounds like you've already done that."

Beth felt her hopes sink. "Is there anything else I can do?"

"Well," the woman hesitated, "you might consider using a medium who may be able to contact the spirit and communicate with it."

"Can you arrange it?" Beth asked immediately. She didn't stop to think of the consequences. She didn't ask about references or take any of the normal precautions. She was so desperate for answers that she was willing to grasp at any straw.

The woman responded, "I have someone in mind. However, you should know, it can be expensive."

"That's fine," Beth countered. She didn't care about the money. She just reached for her calendar. They set up a meeting in two weeks on a day that Beth had no scheduled guests.

In the two weeks that passed, Beth continued to seclude herself from her guests. Her easy smile remained elusive and she kept to herself.

She ran into Tom once.

It was a Tuesday and the morning clouds were low and gray. The weatherman predicted rain by the afternoon. The atmosphere matched Beth's mood and she went outside for a walk.

Tom stood on the porch of the library, sweeping the steps. It wasn't one of his usual chores, but lately he'd found himself full of excess nervous energy.

He missed Beth. He'd called her every day, but she refused his calls. When he stopped by her house, she didn't answer her door. He saw the curtains in her third floor room move, but he never saw her face. He just wanted to talk to her; to explain, but she wouldn't listen.

So, he worked on the book. He was amazed at the speed with which the novel was progressing. He filled pages and pages per day with just the right sentence, exactly the right form. It was almost as if the book were writing itself.

And it was good. Certainly, it was a departure from his typical storyline. Yes, there was a ghost involved; but, it has a personality, a substance, that made it seem more real. The book was softer; with more emotion. He knew that he was creating something very special.

If only he could share it with Beth.

As if she were an apparition, the woman of his thoughts appeared on the sidewalk before him. She was walking with her head down, oblivious to the world around her.

"Beth," he called out, stepping off the front porch.

She looked up at him. Tom paused in mid step. Her face was pale and gaunt, making her blue eyes seem huge in their sockets. She wore a t-shirt that hung loosely on her too thin frame. Her hair was pulled into a loose ponytail, but the vibrant auburn color seemed dim in the overcast light.

He rushed toward her, taking her in his arms. She didn't resist, but she did not return the hug, either.

He held her away from him, keeping his hands on her shoulders, concern showing clearly in his eyes. "How have you been? I've been trying to call you."

She nodded her head, but her eyes remained vague. "I'm fine."

He studied her face and questioned, "Are you sure?"

Nodding, she replied, "Yes." She didn't elaborate or offer even a hint of further explanation.

So, Tom pressed. He was worried about her. She looked terrible, like she hadn't slept in days. He knew that something was bothering her and he would have liked to help. "Have you had any more experiences with Laurilee?"

For the first time, a flash of emotion crossed Beth's face as she answered sharply, "Laurilee is fine."

Properly chastised, Tom took a step back, removing the physical contact between them. "So, you've seen her again?"

She looked at him with hard eyes. "What difference does it make? Or do you need more information for your book?"

"That's not fair," he protested. "I care about you Beth. And I'm worried about you."

"Don't worry about me," she responded and then added cryptically, "I have everything under control."

Tom narrowed his eyes. "What do you mean?"

Beth shook her head, waving him off with her hand. "Never mind."

A bad feeling settled in Tom's gut at her grim tone. He felt his heart race as he asked, "You're not planning anything dangerous, are you?"

Again, the flash in her eyes. "Like I said, don't worry about me. Or Laurilee," she added. "Just worry about your book. How's it coming along, by the way?" Her voice dripped with sarcasm.

Tom answered honestly, "It's coming along very well. I wish you would read it."

"Fat chance," she retorted meanly. "I'm not interested in your lies and half-truths."

"It's called fiction," Tom pointed out. "And you might be surprised." He kept his voice soft and his gaze locked on hers, trying to speak with his eyes all of the emotion that he was unable to utter with his lips--openness, honesty and trustworthiness.

Taking a step away from him, she said quickly, "You've surprised me enough." But, her voice had lost some of its venom.

Tom had witnessed the conflict in her eyes. He had seen her almost open up to him. And then pull away just as quickly. She looked sad again. But, at least the brief rush of emotion had added some color to her cheeks.

Now, he nodded his head gently. "Okay, you win."

He turned and walked back up the porch steps, leaving her standing on the sidewalk. When he reached the porch, he turned, smiling softly at her. "See you around."

She didn't reply. But, she watched him for a long moment before turning and walking away.

Chapter Thirteen

The day of the ghost hunt arrived hot and muggy. Beth stood on the porch feeling her loose cotton shirt stick to her back and shoulders, even as the sun dipped in the horizon. It was late afternoon. An older model blue van sat in her driveway. She watched as four people, two men and two women, unloaded various pieces of equipment onto the lawn. The medium and apparent leader of the group, a middle-aged woman with wire-rimmed glasses and long straight hair name Dena, had been adamant that no one enter the house until all of the preparations were complete. The investigation, as she called it, would begin the instant the group set foot inside the door.

Dena took a moment in the lawn to speak to the group, assigning equipment and dividing the group into teams. One team would investigate the courtyard and surrounding lawn while the other team would head inside the house with Beth. They would meet back on the front porch within the hour.

While half the team walked around the house toward the courtyard, Beth stood next to Dena and her partner, a heavyset man named Phil. Dena said a short prayer asking for protection during the investigation at the entrance of the house and then stepped inside.

"Laurilee won't hurt you," Beth said defensively, following behind Dena. For some reason, the blessing had offended her.

Dena merely shrugged, "You can never know about these things," and continued walking through the house. She held in her hand a camcorder which she used to pan the room. Around her neck hung an elaborate camera and she stopped to take pictures as she walked through the room.

Phil followed behind and kept a log, noting things like air vents and fuse boxes. He also took temperature readings and held out a needle compass that read electromagnetic fields. He noted major appliances and electronics that might interfere with the reading of the compass. Held across his chest with a leather strap, Phil carried a tape recorder with an external microphone.

It seemed very complicated to Beth and she watched closely as the two walked through the downstairs of the house.

Dena shook her head and mumbled, "There's nothing here." Still, she snapped pictures and the tape recorder whirred. Each mumble was recorded in Phil's notebook. He didn't want to mistake his leader's mumblings for any true results.

"You have to go upstairs," Beth offered and was rewarded with a withering look from Dena as Phil scribbled furiously in his notebook.

"Sorry," she whispered and retreated to a corner of the room.

Finally, the group ascended the winding staircase. As they walked through the second floor guestrooms, Beth wondered what images the video camera would pick up. Dena stood at the windows and took pictures of the courtyard. Below, the rest of her team was visible walking through the grounds. In a similar fashion, one team member held a video camera with a digital camera strapped around his neck while the other followed with a pen and notebook, jotting down information as they worked.

Quickly, Dena motioned to move from the second floor to the third floor. Apparently, nothing here had caught her attention.

Beth felt her heart begin to race as the trio mounted the stairs. Her breathing became more and more labored as they grew closer to her room. As soon as they stepped inside, she felt Laurilee's presence. The sweet lavender smell wafted through the air. Beth took a deep breath and let the sweet aroma fill her lungs.

Dena stopped in the middle of the room, standing completely still. Did she sense Laurilee's presence as well?

After a moment, she turned to the nightstand, where the letters sat in a bundle. She reached for the stack.

"No," Beth lunged forward, reaching for the letters. "Don't touch those," Beth said, not realizing that she'd lost her British accent and taken on a southern drawl, nor could she see her own eyes and know that they were radiated with panic.

Dena glanced at her partner, nodding ever so slightly to make sure his tape recorder picked up Beth's words. Phil nodded, understanding instantly, and began making notes.

Dena acquiesced and set the letters down. Beth calmed down immediately and moved to the corner of the room to watch. Dena continued to inspect her surroundings. She moved to stand by Phil, checking the temperature gage.

"Beth," Dena whispered.

When several additional comments failed to break her concentration, Dena grabbed Beth by the arm and pulled her into the hallway.

Beth seemed to blink in confusion. "What's going on?" She held a faded photograph in her hand and rubbed her fingers across its surface almost compulsively.

"We've finished our investigation of your room," Dena replied, staring hard. Then she asked, "Are you all right?"

Beth nodded. "Did you talk to Laurilee?"

Dena shook her head then said. "Our tests were inconclusive."

"Oh, but she was there," Beth protested, "I felt her." Dena started to enter the room again, but Beth continued, "She's gone now."

Dena stopped and turned. "Where is she?"

"The attic," Beth answered in a dreamy voice, starting to zone out again. It was Laurilee's room. The place where she felt most secure.

Dena checked her watch.

Beth stared at the medium as she checked the time, feeling a little put off.

Together, the trio moved up the stairs into the attic. Beth sensed Laurilee waiting for them at the top of the stairs. Once inside the attic, her presence grew stronger, filling the room.

Dena staggered forward, not entirely for show, and clasped her chest. Taking a deep breath, she began her routine by calling out, "Spirit, make yourself known."

There was no movement in the room, but Beth began to move nervously, wringing her hands together.

Turning to Beth, Dena asked, "Where is the picture?"

Beth held out the black and white photo. As Dena reached for the picture, it jerked from Beth's hand and fell to the floor. Beth picked it up quickly and put it back in her pocket. "She doesn't want you to see it."

Dena shrugged and turned back to face the window. "Spirit, I command you to cooperate. Make yourself known."

Beth gasped and paced in agitation. She began to stutter. "Don't talk to her like that. She doesn't like your voice."

"Leave this to me," Dena commanded.

Beth cringed at her tone, biting her lip anxiously. "But, you're scaring her. She won't talk to me if she's scared."

Dena stared at her. "She's an apparition. She doesn't know scared. Don't you want me to remove the apparition from your house?"

A door slammed somewhere in the distance and Dena inclined her head.

Before Beth could reply, Dena said loudly, "Spirit, you must leave this place. Beth no longer wishes to have you present."

As Dena's voice rose abruptly, the drawers in the ancient dresser began to open and shut loudly. Beth ran to the dresser, holding her hands over her ears, calling out blindly, "That's not true."

As soon as Beth reached the dresser, Laurilee moved, pushing a picture off the top of the dresser so that glass shattered onto the wooden floor.

Beth followed, calling, "Laurilee. It's me. Beth. Laurilee."

But the spirit moved through the room, knocking over boxes and slamming dresser drawers.

Over the clattering, Dena continued, "You must leave now. I command you! Leave now!"

"No!" Beth cut her off, shouting and running across the room as the boxes tipped themselves over and clothes scattered across the floor. "Laurilee, don't leave. Talk to me. I want to know about the children."

In her panic, Beth tripped over a trunk and went sprawling onto the floor, cutting her forehead in the process. Blood poured from the gash, running into her eyes, mixing with the tears and blinding her further.

Around her, the room looked as if it had been hit by a tornado. Furniture tumbled over, papers scattered across the floor. Beth sat on the floor, sobbing hysterically. "Laurilee, I'm sorry. Please don't leave."

She held her face in her palms, crying. But, Dena's voice grew stronger, contradicting her; ordering, "You must leave now."

The room became still in an instant. Drawers ceased banging. Boxes settled back into place. Dena stood in the middle of the room, pale.. She turned to Beth with a gleam in her eye. "I think you've heard the last of your apparition."

Tears coursed down Beth's face. She stared blankly in front of her, feeling out of sorts, empty. Then, she held a shaky hand to her mouth and whispered coarsely, "I'm sorry, Laurilee. I just wanted to talk to you." She sobbed for a second and then took a ragged breath. "I didn't mean for this to happen."

Dena raised her eyebrow. "Look, you got what you wanted. The spirit is gone." She wiped her hands one across the other in a gesture of dismissal. "Good riddance, I say."

Beth blinked and turned her head slightly to the right. "No, Laurilee," she whispered, her eyes wide with terror.

Dena's gaze swung in that direction. From the corner of the room, a wooden hat stand rose and leveled itself horizontally. The medium's eyes grew big as the wooden stand floated in her direction, its sharp point aimed directly at Dena's chest.

"Stop," Dena's voice cracked as the stand moved closer. "Stop, I command you."

Gone was the fire and brimstone of earlier; replaced with a genuine fear.

"Laurilee, stop," Beth cried. "Don't do this, Laurilee. You are not that kind of person."

The stand continued its forward movement until the top of the point touched Dena's skin.

Both women held their breath as the levitating hat stand held its position.

One move and the sharp point would pierce the delicate skin above Dena's breastbone.

Dena's face was white and her breaths shallow as she tried to keep her skin from touching the metal point. The woman looked around wildly from the hat rack to the door as if she wanted to run, but didn't know how to get away.

Beth felt paralyzed as well. For the first time, she became fully aware of her surroundings. The anger in the air was almost tangible. Beth had often felt Laurilee's deep sadness; but, she was angry now. Closing her eyes, Beth tried to connect with that anger.

Rising, and crossing the wooden floor, she could feel and see what Laurilee saw--the house, her comfort zone, zoomed out of reach as she stared out the window.

Instead of the courtyard below, Beth saw an ally, dirty and cold, below. She, as Laurilee, was thin and frail and she wore a tattered shawl around her shoulders to keep out the chill from the winter air. Her body was tired and her will broken. All she had left were memories.

A sob escaped her lips at the last memory. One so painful, she felt her heart constrict in her chest. She braced herself against the windowsill; but the memories flooded faster than her body could bear. She sank to the floor in a heap.

Laurilee's last day at the mansion.

"You must leave the house at once." James' words, torn from his lips, but unbending nonetheless. Mattie's cold, pleased smile as she stood next to him.

She hadn't been able to say good-bye to her family. She had been forced to pack her meager belongings and report to Mattie at the gatehouse within the hour.

James had not been present.

Beth shuddered as she witnessed Laurilee's endless walk down the driveway toward the road. The children, her children, were playing in the yard--laughing and singing, carefree. They took no notice of her; but, she studied them as blatantly as she dared, trying desperately to brand their image into her heart.

She remembered Mattie, her smile condescending and pleased, standing on the front porch. Laurilee had served her purpose well, but there was no use for her any longer.

"Oh, Laurilee," Beth whispered, opening her eyes. "It's not like that now. I'm not making you leave."

A screech from Dena called for her attention. As the hat stand poked at Dena's chest, she took baby steps backwards until she was pinned against the wall. Laurilee's anger still pulsated, but not as brightly. Beth smiled a little and said weakly to Dena, "She doesn't like you."

"You are insane," Dena hissed as loudly as she dared. "You need more help than I can provide. Aagh..." she flinched as the hat rack jabbed at her chest again.

"What's going on here?"

Tom's rich, deep voice broke the spell. The hat stand clattered to the floor and the room grew silent.

Ignoring the others in the room, Tom rushed to Beth's side. "You're bleeding."

He looked up at Dena in accusation.

Color rushing to her cheeks, Dena took a shaky step over the hat stand and glared at Beth. "You, and your hat stand," she pointed back at the long wooden stand, "need a whole lot more than a ghost hunter."

She spun around, grabbed her equipment and made a beeline for the door. Her assistant, Phil, who stood rooted to his spot in the corner throughout the events, followed right on her heels.

Beth didn't call out or try to follow. A moment later, she heard the van's engine rev to life and tires squeal across the pavement. She leaned heavily against Tom as he helped her rise to her feet.

Not a word was uttered as Tom took her downstairs and cleansed her wound with antiseptic lotion, placing a small gauze square over the jagged cut. Beth allowed him to tend to her like a child, sitting limply in the chair as he worked around her.

Once the bandage was in place, he lifted her gently and carried her into the parlor, laying her carefully on the couch. He had figured that her bedroom was somehow part of this evening's experience and that she might not be ready just yet to revisit the area.

Reaching for the throw blanket draped across the sofa's arm, he covered her and murmured, "I want you to rest for a little while. I'll be back in a couple of hours with some soup."

"But," she started to protest, except that her head suddenly felt like a lead weight and she seemed to melt into the softness of the sofa.

He touched her cheek gently. "It's okay. I'll be back."

Feeling safely surrounded by his presence, Beth fell asleep.

Chapter Fourteen

Beth woke to find that darkness had settled across the lawn. She raised herself groggily into a sitting position, holding her hand to her forehead, which throbbed unmercifully.

Unable, or at least unwilling, to move any further at this point, Beth sat on the sofa looking out the window.

This afternoon had been quite a failure, in pretty much every way she could imagine. Not only had she not found out the information she was looking for, she had angered Laurilee. Not to mention the fact that she'd looked like a complete fool in front of Tom. She sighed deeply and lowered her head in shame and regret.

How had things gotten so out of control?

A batch of white on the coffee table caught her eye. Someone had left a stack of papers on the corner of the table. She didn't remember seeing it this morning when she'd cleaned, but she must have overlooked it. She reached out and scooped up the stack to see if it was trash or if one of the guests had left something important behind.

FOR LOVE OF LAURILEE

Beth felt her heart start to pound. It was Tom's manuscript. He had left it for her to read.

But, he knew how she felt about his exploitation of Laurilee. How dare he flaunt it in front of her? Did he think a bump on the head would make her forget how strongly she felt about the issue?

She tossed the stack back onto the table; however, she seemed unable to remove her gaze from the manuscript before her.

"I wish you would read it..."

His words fluttered through her memory. She pushed them away. She had been perfectly clear in her response to his request. She refused to read any such garbage about Laurilee. Still, with a will of their own, her arms reached out toward the table.

"...you might be surprised."

She turned the manuscript to face her. Despite the pounding in her head, the words seemed to jump out at her

FOR LOVE OF LAURILEE
By: Sam Shelling

"Read it--for me."

This time the words belonged to Laurilee, spoken in her soft southern accent. Her sweet scent filled the room and Beth looked up, her eyes wide. "Laurilee?"

"It's okay. Read it for me."

Almost trancelike, Beth lifted the cover from the manuscript

When Tom arrived over an hour later, carrying a carton of steaming chicken soup straight from the local diner, he found Beth sitting on the sofa, crying.

"Honey, what happened?" He rushed to her side, taking her in his arms. Then, he saw the manuscript stacked neatly by her side.

He pulled back a little so that he could watch her expression. "You read it."

Silently, Beth nodded.

"What did you think?" He almost hated to ask, but he had to know.

Tears started to run down her cheeks as she murmured quietly, "It's beautiful." Despite her resolve to stay cool no matter what she said, Tom felt his face break into a smile even though the words were an attempt at modesty. "That's only the first few chapters. I still have a lot of work to do on the rest of the book."

"It's so poetic and romantic and suspenseful." Beth spoke from her heart. Then she looked down and said quietly, "Laurilee would be proud."

Tom took the statement for the incredibly high compliment it was intended. He flushed with probably the first true pride in his work he'd felt in years. Beth's opinion meant the world to him. "I promise that the rest of the story will be more of the same."

She met his gaze. "I know it will." Then she sighed wistfully. "It won't be easy, though. We never found out what really happened to Laurilee." Her voice was deep with sadness. "I wish I could have helped her. I never found out what she wanted to know."

"Maybe I can help," Tom said carefully. She was still very fragile, but he couldn't keep any more secrets. "At least a little."

She looked at him, waiting.

"I contacted Matthew Latte."

"James' grandson?" Her eyes grew round.

Tom nodded. "He lives in a retirement home near Atlanta. He spent his life as a bachelor in Atlanta."

Beth took deep, calming breaths. The air was pregnant with tension. She asked in a voice barely higher than a whisper, "What did he say?"

Tom held her gaze. "He said that his father, James' son, was a good man. That he ran the plantation as smoothly as his father. He said that his father was full of life and had a great sense of humor. That no matter how many hours he put in at the plantation, he was home in time to read his children a bedtime story. And that his mother adored him. They were very happy."

"And Samantha?" Beth asked as tears welled in her eyes again. "Did he mention her?"

Tom nodded. "She and Jonathon were very close. She moved to Virginia with her husband, but visited often. They were a lot alike, both spirited and energetic. He said his Aunt Sam was a little more reserved than his father--who apparently loved to pull practical jokes--but she always brought a spark to the house when she visited."

Tom paused for a moment, taking a deep breath.

Beth sensed his hesitation and urged, "Whatever it is--tell me."

"Okay." Tom decided. "I asked Matthew if his father or his aunt ever talked about growing up on the plantation. He said his father's favorite memories were of playing with his sister in the courtyard and that his Aunt Samantha used to talk all the time about one of the servants who used to braid her hair with red ribbons."

Beth's mind raced back to the faded red ribbon she had found in her vanity and its mysterious pull. She felt her heart skip a beat and it took an effort to pull her attention back to the man before her.

She blinked back tears and said aloud, "Do you hear that Laurilee? Your children were happy adults with loving families."

She wasn't sure, but she thought she could detect a faint scent of lavender.

Turning back to her own future, to the man sitting before her, Beth said sincerely, "Tom, I'm sorry. I should have given you a chance." She raised her hand to touch his cheek. "I knew you were a good person. I knew you would never hurt me." She shook her head and stepped away. "I got so caught up in everything. And I was so stubborn…"

"It's okay," Tom stopped her, pulling her back to him. "I should have told you the truth. Believe me, I agonized over it. So many times

I wanted to tell you," he frowned, "but, I couldn't. I've been lost in my own identity crisis. I felt my worth, as a person, without Sam Shelling, was nothing. I didn't want to lose you."

"Oh, Tom," Beth wrapped her arms around him. "Sam is just a persona. He's not real. You are real. And you are wonderful."

She tipped her head back to see him better. Tom held her gaze, electrocuting her with the intensity in his eyes. She felt her heart skip a beat under his stare. Her body grew still as anticipation coursed through her veins. It still amazed her how effortlessly he could change from the easygoing man with the ready smile to this passionate, sexy man who made her weak with desire.

When his lips touched hers, fire coursed through her veins and her knees grew weak. She clung to him, matching his kisses with a mounting desire. She had missed his touch during the time they had been apart. Now, her body leaned towards him, like a tree reaching for the sun.

They kissed, savoring the sweetness of the moment. Beth felt a dizziness that had nothing to do with the bump on her forehead. Never before had the mere touch of a person's lips against hers ignited such a fire. The taste was so exquisite in and of itself that she never wanted to stop, yet her body yearned for the same attention being received by her mouth.

"Beth," he murmured her name against her lips. His breath caressed her lips and mouth. She took in a quick breath as her heart pulsed. He stopped for an instant and then devoured her lips with his own. Beth hung on for dear life. She was riding a wave of emotion so intense it threatened to drown her.

When he moved his hands to the buttons on her blouse, Beth was more than ready. Her skin flamed beneath the thin material and her breasts expanded to meet his touch. His fingers were hot against her skin, creating a spark of electricity that shocked through her body.

While Tom explored the round contours of her breasts with his hands and his lips, she ran her fingers through his thick hair, keeping him close to her skin, never wanting to be apart from his touch. As the caress from his lips sent her into a frenzy, she ripped the shirt from his chest, needing with an unimaginable urgency to press her flesh against his.

He groaned as their skin made contact. The thick mat of hair covering his chest gave way to the hard muscles beneath as Beth pressed the softness of her body against him. He wrapped his arms around her neck and held her tightly, molding her body to his. They fit together perfectly.

As he held her like that, Tom nuzzled through her thick hair to find the tender skin of her neck. He teased and nipped at her skin, sending a pulse of excitement with each gentle nip. She leaned her head to the side, exposing a greater expanse of creamy skin. Her long hair swung out, ringlets cascading around her shoulders. Taking his cue, Tom kissed his way along her neck to where her exposed breasts waited anxiously.

He laid her back gently against the sofa, admiring the perfection of her body. She was thin, yet supple, like a Greek goddess. Her dark hair fanned across the sofa framing her light skin, giving her an ethereal appearance. Lying there so perfectly, she looked pure and untouched.

And then she met his eyes. They smoldered with the desire only a woman could have. She reached for him and pulled him to her. He went willingly.

Their lovemaking was slow and wonderful. An act born of respect and admiration. Tom was careful to be tender. He sensed Beth's vulnerability, but she responded with an ardor that was void of all inhibition.

Her passion fueled his desire and they met in an explosion of fire that warmed to a burning ember as they lay wrapped in each other's arms.

Beth smiled a lazy smile as she stretched out next to him on the sofa. "See, I told you."

Tom leaned up on one elbow and gazed down at her. "Told me what?"

She smiled at him again, not holding back the joy and satisfaction in her eyes. "That you were wonderful."

He blushed and smiled. "Wow. Same to you."

Sighing with deep contentment, he lay back and pulled her to him again. "This is so much nicer than fighting. I'm glad you finally came to your senses."

He was teasing and she knew it. She smiled and turned to him, her blue eyes large and serious. "You have to promise me something, though."

"Anything," he answered immediately.

"No more secrets." She looked like a little girl as she asked and his heart melted.

He hugged her hard and nodded against the top of her head. "I promise. No more secrets."

Then she relaxed against him and laid her head on his shoulder, content.

With his arms tightly around her, Tom asked, "Do you think Laurilee would approve of this?"

"Of us?" Beth asked. "I'm sure she would. From reading her letters it's pretty clear to me that she was a believer of romance and the hope for happy endings."

As she said the words, Beth sat up abruptly.

"What is it?" Tom sat up with her.

She turned to look at him. "Happy endings. Laurilee just needs a happy ending." She held on to his hands. "I need to do one more thing. Can you wait here for me?"

Tom furrowed his eyebrows. "Do you want me to go with you?" He was clearly concerned for her safety, especially after witnessing the destruction from earlier in the day.

But, Beth shook her head. "It's okay." She nodded with encouragement. "I'm okay. I'll be right back."

Although she felt calm and peaceful inside, Beth moved slowly up the stairs to the attic, today's incident too fresh on her mind. The attic was dark, silhouetted only by the moonlight shining in from outside. Still, the effects of Laurilee's rage were apparent. Beth picked up the hat stand and ran her hand along the length of the wood. She set it aside and absently righted a turned-over box and pushed in the drawers from one of the dressers.

Moving to the window, she looked out over the courtyard below, imagining a time long ago, when children played below.

But, she lived in the present now and the future was bright. It was time to put the past to rest.

"Laurilee," her voice was strong, but quiet, "I'm your friend. I want to help you. I know that you didn't want to give up your children…"

"The children."

The words floated across the room. Beth didn't turn from the window and she didn't let the words inside, but she closed her eyes and spoke aloud.

"They were happy." Beth spoke quietly into the room. "Your grandson, Matthew, is alive. He said that his father, your son, led a full and happy life. He ran the plantation and married the girl of his dreams. And Samantha, your daughter, married and moved to Virginia. Matthew said she used to speak of a servant girl who braided her hair with a red ribbon…"

Beth stopped as tears ran down her cheeks. "You should find them, Laurilee. You and James. James died of a broken heart after you left. He loved you. He did."

She cleared her throat and said, "Go and find them now. Be a family. There is no one left here."

Beth felt Laurilee's warmth tighten around her for a brief second. Beth cocked her head, listening to the voice from within and then nodded in reply.

After that, Laurilee was gone.

Beth opened her eyes and looked out over the courtyard below. The moonlight shone brightly over the lush yard and the smell of lavender floated through the open window.

Beth smiled. The smell would always remind her of Laurilee.

As she walked down the stairs, Beth felt safe in the warm blanket of love and peace. Laurilee was not a threat to this house, she had been a blessing.

Beth walked quietly into the living room and smiled. Tom had fallen asleep on the sofa, his head leaning against the armrest, the blanket covering him from the waist down. His thick hair fell over his forehead in a wave. Beth knelt down before him and stared at his face. His skin was smooth and unlined and his lips curved into a half smile. She smiled, too, and reached out to touch his cheek. It was cool and soft and she left her hand there, enjoying the contact.

Her own body felt peaceful and she knew that she had changed her own life in a significant way.

After a second, Tom stirred. He opened sleepy eyes and stared at her. "You're back."

Smiling, she nodded.

Tom sat up and rubbed his eyes. "Is everything okay?"

"She's gone." Beth smiled sadly, but her eyes held a peace that had not been present earlier.

Laurilee was gone, but she'd left one final request for Beth to carry out and Beth intended to make sure it was handled properly.

Chapter Fifteen

"...after Laurilee left the plantation, it was hope, and nothing else, that kept her going. As the years passed with no word from James and no contact with her children, Laurilee's hope began to fade, as did her will to live. She grew old and withered before her time. But, the hope she clung so desperately to followed her into death. She couldn't let go." Beth finished relating her story to Tom as they sat at her kitchen table, drinking coffee. "That's why she came back to the house--she needed to know that her purpose in life had been fulfilled."

Tom shook his head, "That is an amazing story."

At Beth's unusual request, he had taken some notes, but mostly he had just listened as she had pieced together Laurilee's story from her memories, the letters, and some instinct she couldn't quite qualify. Two hours had passed while Beth spoke and he listened, mesmerized. It was better than a story--it was real.

"There is one thing I don't understand," he commented, rubbing his chin. "If James loved her so much, why did he force her to leave?"

"He didn't have a choice." Beth's expression changed. She looked sad and her eyes filled with tears. It was one of the most painful memories she had experienced through Laurilee. "James Latte had to banish her from the house when she turned twenty-five. Her children were nine and six."

"Why?" Tom frowned and then, just as quickly, nodded in understanding. "House maids weren't allowed to stay in the house once they reached a certain age."

"Unless they had special talents, like being a cook or nanny, the house servants were to be young and pretty," Beth corroborated. "Twenty-five was actually pretty old for a house servant. She wouldn't have been kept around for that long if not for James."

"How sad for her," Tom sighed. "Banished not only from her lover, but from her family. No wonder she left Garden Ridge."

Beth nodded sadly. "Atlanta was the furthest ticket she could afford. She did try to make a decent life for herself. She had been given her freedom when she was released, but she didn't have any skills. She did odd jobs for a while, but barely made ends meet. She finally died in a halfway house."

"What about James? Did he ever try to contact her?" Tom, too, had come to believe in James' love for the servant girl.

Beth shrugged, "I know that Laurilee never saw James or the children again once she left the house."

"That's too bad." Tom could only imagine the heartache of losing his true love. He had come to believe that James and Laurilee were in love and he knew that nothing or no one could ever keep him away from the woman he loved. "I wish he could have found a way to make people accept Laurilee."

"Times didn't change fast enough for James and Laurilee," Beth corrected quietly, for once being the voice of reason. "Remember, he died only five years after Laurilee left."

"With no history of illness," Tom continued, remembering the information they had found in Atlanta. He looked at her, his expression serious. "Do you know what I think?"

"What do you think?" Beth smiled a little and raised her eyebrows at him. Tom's creative energy was flowing. She could see it in the spark of his eye. She had filled in some of the facts and he was weaving a story out of all of the information stored in his memory. Now, he was taking the story along its natural course to see where it would end. Things were progressing right on schedule.

Tom smiled softly in answer to her question. "I think that dying was the only way for James to truly show his love for Laurilee. I think that James and Laurilee are together in death in a way that they could never be allowed in life."

"I think maybe you're right," Beth agreed, trying to hide her smile. He was right on target.

Tom sighed, "What an amazing story."

Now Beth grinned at him. "A bestseller, I would think."

Frowning, Tom stared at her. "What do you mean?"

Beth regarded Tom with a mischievous glint in her eye. "Laurilee asked one final favor before she left."

"Really? What kind of favor?" Tom asked, intrigued. She hadn't mentioned anything of the sort during their whole conversation.

"A favor from you, actually." Beth's smile sparked a little.

"Me?" Tom cocked his head to one side. "I thought she didn't like me."

Beth laughed now. "Well, maybe the message isn't exactly for you. Maybe it's for Sam Shelling. You'll have to decide."

"What do you mean?" Tom looked confused.

Beth blushed a little, but said proudly, "Her last words to me were to ask you to tell her story. And, since we really don't know the ending, you might have to fill it in."

Tom lifted an eyebrow. "She's not afraid of what I might write?" And, by she, they both knew he meant Beth.

Now Beth laughed for real. "Well, she did mention that she'd be right next to you to make sure you got it right."

Tom made a face and then laughed for a moment with her. But, he turned to her in an instant with a serious expression. "Do you think I can do it? I mean for real?"

The insecurities of years of writer's block weighed on him.

She reached out and smoothed her palm across his skin. "Let me put it this way," Beth said quietly, but with a firmness that surprised them both. "I don't think you need Sam Shelling to write it for you."

Tom's eyes widened and he exhaled sharply. "Wow. Sam and I have been together for a long time. I'm not sure I know how to write without him."

Beth reached out her hand to him. "I read what you wrote. Those were the words of Tom Hartman, not Sam Shelling."

"But, what about my fans?" He grimaced. "I mean Sam's fans?"

"They'll love you just as much," Beth announced firmly.

Tom looked at her with an agonized expression. "How can you be so sure?"

Beth held his gaze with her clear blue eyes and smiled, "Because I love you just as much."

Tom moved back to the table to sit beside her, cupping her face in the palms of his hands. "You love me?"

Beth nodded, her face full of joy and relief.

Tom leaned forward and took her in his arms. Holding his face merely inches from her, he whispered against her lips, "I'm so glad."

His kiss was warm and gentle, a caress against her lips. Beth pulled him in closer, wanting to keep him beside her forever. In response, he wrapped his arms around her, enveloping her with his warmth, pressing his chest against the softness of her breasts.

Beth drew in a breath. The contact with her sensitive skin made her nipples pucker and harden with desire.

Tom drew back for a moment, looking at her. His eyes were intense and his lips full. She smiled at him and he smiled back. In an instant, his lips found hers once more. He kissed her now, possessively, as if, by that one look, he had made her his own.

And he had.

Not by one look; but, by months of sharing and caring and building a foundation that would last them through good times and bad, sickness and health, richer or poorer…

Beth couldn't help but smile.

"What?" Tom drew away at the movement of her lips, regarding her quizzically.

"Nothing." Beth blushed and looked away.

"Hey," he admonished, but very softly. "We're not supposed to have any more secrets. Your rule, remember?"

How could she forget? More heat filled her face as she said truthfully, "I was practicing wedding vows in my head."

If what she said shocked him, it didn't show on his face. Instead, a soft smile spread across his lips and he asked in a very sexy voice, "How did they sound?"

Beth shrugged, feeling her cheeks flame, but unable to suppress a small satisfied smile. "Pretty good, actually."

Tom kissed the tip of her nose and then stood up, taking a step away from her. "There is still one thing, though."

Beth tilted her head to one side and raised her eyebrows in silent question.

"Sam Shelling," Tom clarified, his tone taking on a serious note. "He's still a part of me, no matter what happens with this book. I am Sam Shelling and I write ghost stories."

Beth had thought about Sam Shelling a lot over the past weeks. She hated him for taking Tom away from her. She loved him for adding to the creative person that she loved in Tom. She knew in her heart that one would be lost without the other.

Smiling softly at him, she answered his question. "If Sam Shelling is anything like Tom Hartman, I'll love him just as much."

Tom smiled back at her and took her in his arms. His voice lightened considerably as he joked, "Actually, Sam is nothing like me. He's quite a snob."

"Oh, my," Beth raised her head, her eyes twinkling. "What will Sam think of you dating a lowly owner of a bed and breakfast? It's not very glamorous, you know."

"That's true." Tom rested his chin against the top of her head. "Can we just tell him that you're a famous ghost hunter? That will really impress him."

Beth groaned, the sound muffled by Tom's shirt, and he laughed. Then he pulled away to look at her again. He voice was warm with emotion. "Thank you, Beth, for giving me another chance."

Beth smiled back. "I should be thanking you for being so persistent."

"Actually, we should both probably thank Laurilee for bringing us together in the first place." Tom smiled at her.

"You're right." Beth grinned and then looked out the window towards the courtyard. "Thank you, Laurilee."

As the couple stood in the kitchen enfolded in a loving embrace, a star twinkled brightly in the night and the smell of lavender filled the air.

If you enjoy a good story full of romance and mystery, you'll love the writing of TrishAnn Williams. Her stories feature strong heroines and a hero that always comes through in the end.

As an active member of both local and national chapters of Romance Writers of America, she enjoys taking an idea and weaving a creative, memorable story around it

TrishAnn Williams has been writing romance novels for many years. In 1994, two of her novelettes, one a romantic suspense and one a contemporary romance, were published by Cogswell Publishing.

TrishAnn's first published novel, HAUNTING AT LAURILEE INN, is scheduled for release by Parker Publishing in early 2012. The idea for Haunting at Laurilee Inn was inspired by one of the colorful historic stories told in a French Quarter ghost tour that TrishAnn attended when she lived in New Orleans.

TrishAnn resides in Austin, Texas with her husband, Mark, her twin boys, Luke and Logan and her dog Emmitt.

For more information on TrishAnn Williams, please visit her website at TrishAnnWilliams.com

CPSIA information can be obtained at www.ICGtesting.com
Printed in the USA
LVOW131528130912

298697LV00012B/98/P